ONE SPRING IN PARIS

Published by Sapere Books.

20 Windermere Drive, Leeds, England, LS17 7UZ,
United Kingdom

saperebooks.com

ISBN: 978-1-913518-69-1

CHAPTER I

In the New Year, when Raoul Pierre was in his apartment convalescing after an attack of *la grippe*, he foolishly confided in his friend Georges, known as the lightest-hearted man in Paris, that he was 'fed-up' with everything. This was surprising, for Raoul was young, handsome and rich. He owned the 'Maintenon', an exclusive restaurant on the left bank of the Seine, which was renowned throughout the world for its excellent cuisine and fine wines. After visiting Paris, travellers who had not eaten at the 'Maintenon', and sampled its excellent cellars, were told that they had not seen Paris, and that their education was incomplete.

It did not occur to Georges, who had never had a day's illness in his life, that the depression after flu is worse than the illness itself. He had one cure for all man's ills. Georges looked knowingly at his friend, who was sitting languidly in a deep armchair, dressed in a silk, many-hued dressing-gown, and said: "What is wrong with you is that you have no direction in your life, no incentive to live, no woman on whom to lavish gifts you can well afford. You are high, wide and handsome, and eligible as few men under thirty are nowadays, and you keep it all selfishly to yourself because you do not know any better, and no one has told you the truth about yourself."

"Oh, is that how I seem to you? If I have a fortune it is because I have worked hard to make it."

"But you haven't the faintest idea how to spend it."

"On a bevy of strange women who will like me for what I can give them?" was the sarcastic question.

"No, my good friend. I do not wish you ill but well. Spend your considerable savings on *one* woman."

"Where is she to be found? On the boulevards? In the Bois under the limes? Up in the air like an angel?"

"Now you are being really foolish and uncooperative. You will of course choose the lady from among your friends."

"I have no time for friends like that."

"What an excuse! You must *make* time. It will be worthwhile, I assure you. Loneliness is another name for bachelor-sickness."

"What nonsense you talk, Georges! You are taking advantage of my temporary weakness to push your silly ideas on to me. It is *my* life you are flinging to the women. I am not like you, blithely offering my heart on a platter to my friends, wherever they may be, and taking it back the next day. It is beyond me to pick a wife like that, just as though you are picking a flower. Besides, I should, without your nimble experience of women, pick a dud. That would indeed be terrible. No, I could not take such a risk. It would be asking too much of Fate."

"Perhaps you are looking for that perfection in a wife which you aim at in your restaurant?"

"Maybe. I have learned that it is attention to detail that counts. You must agree with me there?"

Georges nodded, and tried to look wise. As he had a comic cast of face he looked silly. He said: "When I think how rich you are I do agree: but millions of francs made from appealing to people's senses and stomachs do not make for a man's happiness, though they do so swell his bank balance. To win happiness you must touch the human heart."

"So that's what you are driving at! You want me to fall in love. You are too sentimental, Georges."

"I am being practical." Then Georges glanced at his wristwatch and jumped to his feet. "I must go. I have an appointment this evening — a special one." He laughed self-consciously. "I would not be late for it for worlds." Then he added defiantly, "I do not expect you to believe me, but this time it is the real thing."

Raoul laughed. "I have heard all that before. The repetition of your love theme wearies me."

"Only because you are not in love yourself. Indeed, I am beginning to think you are too selfish, too wrapped up in yourself, too sorry for yourself being ill, ever to fall in love. But let me tell you it would take you into another world. You would forget your ego, something I can see that the great Raoul Pierre would never wish to do."

"Go on," urged Raoul grimly as Georges paused for breath. "It is my friend speaking."

"I have caught your attention. So. Of course you would not be able to give so much time and thought to your business as you do now, if you were in love. You would be too occupied making the girl love you to be absorbed in such mundane things as food and drink. For I believe, under the cold veneer of polish you wear so nicely and which makes you *oh so attractive* to women, you are hiding the fires of a volcano, which once roused you would never succeed in quenching. If you fell in love…" Georges paused dramatically, then he smiled, shrugged and spread out his hands. "But there, it must remain a pipe-dream, for you would want such perfection in a woman as does not exist."

There was some truth in Georges' words, and Raoul said mildly: "You know me so well, surely in your wanderings you have met just the type of girl to suit my fastidious taste. It would be most interesting to meet her."

7

"Not if you meet her in your present mood. It would be fatal for both of you." Georges took the invalid's hand in his. "Don't worry, Raoul. *When* I find this paragon for you I'll bring her along."

"I'm not worrying," said Raoul, offhandedly, and was glad that Georges was going.

Raoul soon forgot this foolish talk. He went home for a fortnight to stay with his father, the Marquis de la Fallière, who was living in the only habitable corner of the ruined Château Candide which, as every tourist knows, is in the Loire district of France. When the prunus and almond trees were in pink and white blossom in the Bois, and the plane trees along the boulevards in Paris were bursting into leaf, Raoul, fit and ready for work, returned to Paris.

He was still vaguely depressed about something, though he could not put a name to this inner unease of mind and spirit. Being well, when he met Georges, Raoul was not such a fool as to confide further in his friend.

Georges was in fine fettle. He overflowed with *bonhomie* and high spirits.

"I can see that you are in love again," Raoul said tolerantly.

"Not again. I am *still* in love. I told you it was the real thing."

"Do I know her?"

"I brought her here, but you were away. You do not know her. She is an American, over here to study art."

"Then I bet she keeps you on your toes. That will be a good thing for you, Georges. It will steady you. I am glad for your sake."

"And you?"

"Yes?" Raoul inquired, puzzled. "What about me?"

"You have not met the perfect one?"

"I have not looked. Did you think I would? You must be crazy."

"Then I must do it for you."

"Let me know when you find her," said Raoul lightly, then as the telephone shrilled he picked up the receiver saying: *"Pardon... 'Allo. 'Allo!"* and straightway forgot Georges' existence in a long-distance call to Nice about some mimosa that had been promised but had not arrived. "I must have it. Send it by air. This is spring. People expect blossom and bird song and lambs in spring."

Georges crept out of the room, thinking, *He's forgotten love — people fall in love in the spring.*

A week later, when there were banks of mimosa, a froth of yellow fluff, in the foyer of the 'Maintenon', Georges brought Fanny to lunch and introduced her with some trepidation to Raoul. He was very much in love, young and jealous. He knew that though Raoul held himself aloof from all women, that very attitude, coupled with his wealth and good looks, was probably the reason for a great part of his phenomenal success — for it is human to hold out the hands to the ripest plum just out of reach.

Fanny was blonde, blue-eyed and petite. She was sure of herself, vivacious, and beautifully dressed. Yet Georges' jealous eyes could see that for some unknown reason she held no appeal for Raoul. Perhaps there was some truth in the rumour that Raoul had no heart?

"You like her?" he asked Raoul anxiously at the first chance.

"Mademoiselle is charming," agreed Raoul. Then he added kindly, with the authority of an elder brother: "But don't get too involved. These rich Americans are not greatly enamoured of a poor man who is only a Foreign Office clerk. You may be useful as an escort, but remember, the lady is rich and lovely. It is obvious that you will have great competition for her heart and hand."

"That's what I am afraid of," said Georges glumly, hating to hear his secret fears put into words.

"And that," said Raoul unfeelingly, "is what keeps you in love. Well, you've been steady for a month now. May it last."

"Oh, you and your advice!" Georges flung at him.

It was natural for Fanny to ask questions about Raoul. "Does he like me?"

"Raoul hates blondes."

"Oh! Why?" Fanny bridled with anger, but having glanced at herself in a convenient mirror she was quickly reassured. No one could hate her.

"I do not know, unless it is that when he was studying at Grenoble, Raoul fell for a blonde. She let him down. It was calf-love. Raoul is clever, a genius, but perhaps his heart is suffering from retarded development, because he never seems to have forgotten the hurt he had when a calf."

"All blondes are not alike. Anyway, gentlemen are supposed to prefer them," pouted Fanny.

"In the book, but not in real life," asserted Georges. "*Some* blondes can be tough, though." Then hastily and with tact, Georges added: "I do not mean you, *chérie*. You are sweet."

But Fanny was annoyed with Raoul. He had not attacked her personally, but she was among the legion of blondes that Raoul hated. She said darkly: "Your friend is too sure of himself. One day he'll meet his match."

"I sincerely hope so. Raoul is overdue for a shake-up. He is too complacent, sitting on a growing pile of money. It is disgusting to think of such a young man with all that money, and no woman in his life to spend it for him."

Fanny was quiet for five minutes. She was thinking hard. Her eyes were remote and brooding. Then she threw a bombshell at Georges. "Do you think he would like my friend?"

"Who? Caroline? Oh, no, she's blonde, too. Raoul would not look at her."

"Caroline is not blonde. She is auburn. That is different. But I forgot. Caroline goes back to England when her six months here are up. She's returning like a bad farthing."

"If she wants to stay," said Georges kindly, "I can wangle an extension."

"She can't. Caroline has come to the end of the money her aunt provided for her to study art and languages in Paris. Julian doesn't teach painting for nothing, nor are the Sorbonne lectures for languages free. It just can't be done. My, is Caroline sick about it!"

"I understand that because her father is a poor country parson with a large family she has to stay away."

"Oh, Caroline won't go home. She'll have to get a job at a school in England."

"What a shame! She is a lovely girl, much too good to be boxed up in a school."

"That's what I think."

"Could she not get a job here — a part-time sort of job which would provide the money for her stay here, and pay for her lessons?" suggested Georges hopefully.

"What?"

"I must think — that is, if Caroline really wishes to stay in Paris."

"Caroline adores Paris."

That night, Georges thought of a plan, and wondered why it had not occurred to him before. His only excuse was that he had been too absorbed in Fanny Cornell to think much about Caroline May.

"Eureka!" he cried so loudly in the middle of the night, that he wakened a woman in the apartment below him, who complained to the janitor in the morning that Georges kept her awake all night.

At the moment when she was making her complaint, Georges arrived to see Raoul in his exotic office on the top floor of the "Maintenon'. It was reached by a steep staircase or a private lift.

Raoul was guarded by a woman secretary, one Nini Dogas, who epitomized all that Georges knew of the little French girl of the boulevards. She was thin as a pole, dark-eyed, with a fuzz of black hair, a tip-tilted nose and a large red gash of a mouth. Her black skirt was wrapped about her legs like a swaddled flagpole. Her heels were the highest that could be bought in Paris. She did not walk. She *could* not. Nini teetered around the room, giving a good imitation of a French girl wearing a restrictive Japanese kimono.

Raoul had long ago forgotten his first impression of Nini. Now he liked her. She was a sound business woman. She made few mistakes. Raoul had no patience with fools.

Georges was privileged, as an old friend, to enter the sacred office whenever he liked. As he strode into the room now, Raoul had just finished a telephone conversation, and was replacing the receiver.

"Oh, hello! What do you want at this time of day?" Raoul asked casually, glancing keenly at Georges, observing that as his face was happy he was not wallowing in despair about some love affair. Raoul opened a box of cigarettes and pushed it towards his friend, saying: "What can I do for you? I can give you exactly ten minutes."

"I have come to offer you something." Georges sat down and took a cigarette.

"Something for sale?"

"I am not a slave dealer." Georges lit a cigarette and settled himself in his chair. What he had to say would take longer than ten minutes.

"Oh, what is it?" inquired Raoul, glancing covertly at his wristwatch.

"A girlfriend. No —" as Raoul shook his head decidedly — "wait until I've finished. Do you remember telling me when you were ill that you were 'fed-up', and I replied that you should fall in love and marry?"

Raoul frowned. "Yes, I recall we talked a lot of nonsense at that time. Well?"

"I've found her."

Raoul did not answer. His eyes widened a little as he stared at his friend. "Then keep her!" he cried arrogantly.

"I can't. There's Fanny. She is tops with me. You know that."

"Then lose the girl — do what you like, but don't bring her near me."

Georges was surprised at this answer. He had not expected such a rebuff. It hurt his feelings. "You should be glad, not annoyed." Then he said slowly and deliberately, "I can only suppose you are afraid to meet Miss May."

Raoul whitened and jumped to his feet. "No man shall call me a coward," he said with quiet fury in his voice. "Not even you."

"I shouldn't dream of calling you one. You are not. Your worst enemy could not say that, and I am your best friend.

Pistols for two and coffee for one doesn't come into the picture for you and me. But in an important matter of the heart, such as this, I can't let it drop easily. This is vital."

"Explain yourself," Raoul sat down and said stiffly.

"What I meant was that *subconsciously* you were afraid to meet Miss May, in case you fell in love with her. You don't want that to happen, but it might and it could — if you met the girl."

"I suppose she is an American friend of Miss Cornell's?" Raoul asked, doodling with a pen on blotting paper.

"No, Caroline is English. They share a room in Montmartre. It isn't much of a place because, though Fanny has dollars enough to live in luxury, Caroline is the daughter of a country parson with a large family. They are as poor as church mice. Caroline is dreadfully poor."

"So you want me to provide her with money. Is that it? And in return she will love me and cure me of my fits of depression, so that I shall not be 'fed-up' but 'full up'? The answer is no. You do not understand the type of fellow I am, Georges. I am disappointed in you." Raoul glanced at the ornate French clock on the shelf above the electric fire panel. It was lit though it was spring, for Mademoiselle Dogas, who sat at a little table in a corner of the room, out of earshot, yet near enough to play chaperon to any lady visitors, was often cold. She suffered from poor circulation, and her chilblains did not disappear until the early summer.

Georges took no notice of the hint, and remained seated. "It is you who do not understand: it is I who should be shocked, dismayed and wretched because you think so low of me — your friend. I am not offering you a beggar or a slave, but a girlfriend, a nice girl who has a sound 'roast beef' background, sweet, simple and charming. Don't turn it down easily."

Raoul was silent. He forgot to draw lines and hooks on his blotting paper. His pencil remained poised in still fingers, and his eyes were fixed on the bright mimosa in a vase on his desk. Long ago, his father had begged him to settle down in life, and obediently Raoul had reviewed the list of his girlfriends. Not one had appealed to him. There might be a grain of wisdom in what Georges hinted. These feather-brained chaps sometimes framed a bright idea.

Raoul raised his eyes to Georges' face. They were moody, but showed that he was ready to listen further.

Georges said, "I suggest you offer her a post — a part-time job on your staff, so that you may have daily contact with Miss May and get to know her when you will fall for her and want her as your wife."

Raoul's face flushed with deep anger. "How dare you sit there and make such a suggestion to me! I do not wish to win a wife from my staff. What do you suggest she shall do here — play chef, or *maîtresse d'hôtel* — or cloakroom attendant — or what? Bah! You and your crack-brained ideas! You try my patience too far. There are limits to joking." Raoul looked impatiently at his wristwatch. "I shall have to turn you out," he said bluntly.

"You have heard me so far, and I can see that my idea has struck you —"

"Nearly flat!" interrupted Raoul. "You are merely stupid, and we will say no more. You have allowed your good nature to run away with your discretion. We will leave it at that."

"If you will only have patience to listen to it all."

Raoul sighed with resignation. Georges bored him. "Go ahead, get it off your chest. You will never be able to do this with me again."

"All right. I am a practical man, and my ideas are original, but *always* fruitful of good results."

Raoul jeered. "Do you call it a good idea for me to take a learned girl from the Sorbonne, and one who studies art under Julian, on my staff? It could not be worse. My staff would go on strike, while I should probably go mad."

"Not if you took Miss May on as a kind of liaison officer."

"What *do* you mean? Is this a game you want me to play?"

"You are known to have a passion for perfection of detail. It is supposed to be the keynote of your success. Anything to further that object would be accepted. Use Miss May to receive and study complaints on both sides, to smooth the ruffled feathers of a client who feels he is being rooked too much over his bill. Let her be free to talk to foreigners in their own language. She is a good linguist, has a smattering of several languages, and speaks some well. She can be here at lunch and dinner-time, while you are open to clients. *Make* the post for her."

"So!" Raoul looked thoughtful. He was quick to catch on to anything good for his business. There might be something in *this* idea. He was silent for a long time, then he banged the desk with his fist. "*Bon Dieu!* I believe you have something there!" he cried. He was not thinking of the girl to fill this new post, but of the improvement such a person could make to his business. Already his nimble mind was looking at this new idea from all angles.

Georges looked smugly down his nose. "I told you it was a first-class idea," he said with relief.

"It *is* good. I shall use it," said Raoul, then remembered why Georges had made the suggestion, and added darkly, "But do not run away with any sentimental thoughts that I am to fall in love with this lady. You know me well enough to be aware that

I am not the sort of man to fall for a stranger out of the blue, someone chosen by my friends not because she would be my choice but because they want me to have her. I have not the time to waste on love."

"You don't want to be friends with a lovely girl?" Georges inquired in astonishment.

"Frankly, no. I am a busy man."

"Too busy for love?"

"*Certainement.*"

Georges shook his head. "You are in bad shape. Something must be done for you by your friends, and quickly. What if I tell you that Caroline May is beautiful as a dream?"

"I never dream."

"That she has hair like burnt copper, full of light and flame; a skin of peaches, and —"

"Green or brown eyes make no appeal to me," was the definite reply.

"Caroline's eyes happen to be grey!" cried Georges triumphantly.

"Oh, well, that's a change."

"It is fascinating. Her lips are sensitive and —"

"That is enough. I do not want you to enumerate the lady's charms. I can only repeat I am not interested. I once knew a blonde who was faithless, and a redhead who was dumb, and a dark-haired girl whose eyes were fixed continuously on my wallet. So I was taught while young to lump all women under one heading and concentrate on my business. You will admit that I now have my reward."

Georges shook his head. "You are missing a lot," he said sorrowfully.

"Perhaps, but as I do not realize that, it does not matter."

Then Georges began to laugh softly at first and then loudly.

"What's so funny?" asked Raoul.

"You; one of these days you are going to wake up — it will be the instant when you fall hard and good for one girl."

"I shall never fall good and hard for anyone."

"That sounds like a challenge to Fate."

"Call it what you like." Raoul shrugged. Then he rose abruptly. "Now, you really must go, Georges. Thank you for the idea. I may be able to do something for your friend's friend. I will think it over, anyway."

"Let me know soon."

"Why is there so much hurry?"

The two friends walked towards the door.

"Because for Miss May the cash is running out. If she does not find a part-time job sufficient to keep herself in Paris and to pay for lectures and lessons, she will return to England."

"The best for her," said Raoul heartily.

The two men shook hands.

"Then you'll let me know first thing in the morning?" said Georges.

"About six o'clock?"

"Nothing wakes me before eight," was the firm reply.

"I am not a philanthropist."

"Miss May would not like that. But —"

"All right, I'll give you a ring at eight in the morning."

"You're a good sort, Raoul," said Georges, wringing his friend's hand.

"Because you want something? The praise is empty!"

CHAPTER II

On the other side of Paris on the heights of Montmartre, Fanny Cornell, a honey blonde, blue-eyed, and with a reckless mouth, whose father was the wealthy owner of a Boston daily paper, and Caroline May, daughter of a country parson of a poor living in the wilds of Norfolk, shared an apartment on the top floor of a tall shuttered house overlooking a courtyard off the rue Tino.

Fanny had just taken off her hat and kicked off her shoes. She had come in from seeing her friend, Georges, a young Frenchman employed at the Foreign Office. He had been excited about a wonderful new part-time job he was trying to secure for Caroline. Fanny guessed it was with Raoul Pierre. She was to sound Caroline about accepting it, and if she showed any unwillingness to impress upon her not only that jobs for English girls did not grow as readily as blackberries in autumn, but this particular job was a snip with a man of fame, and would quickly be snapped up if it were known generally that he was offering it.

Fanny lit a cigarette and threw herself down on her bed, saying, "I'm tired. The vibrant atmosphere of Paris in spring, and the gay enchantment of any pleasure it can offer, *is* tiring, even though I am enjoying every minute of it. How's that sound to you, honey?"

"I gather from that you have been dancing?" said Caroline drily.

Fanny waited to blow a smoke ring into the air. "You have guessed right, honey. But that is the way I like it — 'burning every candle at both ends' as hard as I can."

"I love Paris, too," said Caroline. "If I have to leave here I shall be wretched. Whatever happens I shall always adore Paris."

"Who doesn't?" said Fanny, and turned her head to look at Caroline, aware afresh of the dreamy abstraction in Caroline's grey eyes. She added, "You don't have to go." And she thought slyly, *Now it's time to turn on the works.*

"Well —"

"If it is only dollars…" Fanny drawled with her slow Southern accent.

"That, and my permit, which is nearly up."

"I've told you it will be easy to get an extension. Georges will get it for you."

"A permit for nothing would be silly. Lessons cost money."

"I am tired of telling you to call on me."

"That is generous of you, but I can't accept. You ought to know me better than that."

"*Won't* accept. You are pig-headed, honey."

"Well, won't, if you like."

Fanny smiled at the smoke rings she was blowing into the air. "A girl with your looks need not worry overmuch about getting a job," she said.

Caroline let that pass. She would have been blind not to know that everywhere she went in Paris she attracted attention. But Fanny was sure that it was as much Caroline's personality, her air of repose, and her dignified demeanour which fascinated men in this city of reckless light and laughter, as her glorious colouring.

"Georges has just told me that his friend has a vacancy for you in his restaurant. You must have heard of it — the 'Maintenon'."

"What sort of a job is it?" asked Caroline quickly. She had heard of the famous restaurant.

Georges had been vague. Even the offer of the job was uncertain. Fanny guessed that with Caroline a proposition must be a fact. To arouse her interest Fanny drew on her imagination. It was easy to do this. In her way, Fanny was a great artiste. When she had finished, she said, "Well, what do you think of it?"

"It sounds vague. This man isn't offering me charity?" Caroline questioned.

"What makes you think that? As the daughter of a parson who has wallowed in poverty I am surprised at your inadaptability."

"Well, why in the world should a famous restaurant offer an unknown quantity like myself a job? What could I do there? I can't cook or wait or book-keep — I should be a laughing-stock and feel a fool."

"Oh, there are many side jobs which are quite important in building up a successful business," said Fanny airily. "As for feeling a fool, that, of course, is up to you."

"But it is already successful. Surely even you, Fanny —"

"There is always room for improvement," was the inexorable reply.

"Well, I can't take it, whatever it is. The idea is impossible!"

"Why not? You are too particular, and if you want to stay in Paris you can't afford to be."

"There's something fishy about it."

"Not at all. Are you accusing my Georges of —"

"No, but I do know that Georges has the knack of being lyrical over trifles."

"Caroline!"

"It is no good being reproachful. The job, whatever it is, doesn't ring true. This restaurant may be all right, but *he* sounds all wrong."

"Oh, Raoul isn't an ordinary restaurant-keeper. He is the Comte de Tours."

"And restaurant-keeping is a farce."

"Not a farce, nor a hobby, but a means of living. Raoul may be a member of the old French nobility, but he is self-made. He has built up a world-renowned restaurant business. He has a passion for finding improvements. He will never be satisfied with anything but perfection. I don't know much about this job for you, for it has not been offered yet. There is only talk of it at present. Plans are up in the air. But I do know that Raoul Pierre would not take you or anyone into the business unless he was sure that the business would benefit by you. As a person you do not exist for Raoul. You never will. When you enter his employment you will cease to be human, but only a cog in his machine. Georges is going to give me a ring tomorrow to make an appointment for you to see Raoul. Give me a time for the date."

Caroline hesitated. She felt rather foolish now that Fanny had explained the position. "What is the Comte like?" she asked in a quieter tone of voice.

"They don't call him the Comte in business. He is just M'sieur Pierre. He is old and bald, probably well-married with a dozen kids."

These facts seemed to make up Caroline's mind. "What time will suit him?" she asked with sudden determination.

"Just after the restaurant closes at six, or at nine o'clock I should think." Secretly Fanny was overjoyed that she had cajoled and browbeaten Caroline into wanting this job.

"Either hour will suit me."

"Then make it nine o'clock. He will be good-tempered and more amenable at that hour."

Caroline went over to the open window and looked out. Far below the square window, in the middle of a cobble-stoned yard which was surrounded by tall and short houses whose pink-plastered facades were all more or less scarred and decayed, was a cherry tree in bloom. Someone had hung a canary in a small cage on the wall outside his window. It had been singing all day in the spring sunshine. It was quiet now, hopping about its cage, probably waiting to be taken in for the night.

Sounds of life came into the room from the inhabitants around the courtyard, and the rumble of heavy lorries moving to and from the railway depot at the end of the rue Tino.

Someone was practising singing exercises. She had high, piercing top notes. Just below was the raucous scraping of a violin, whanging across the singer's arpeggios — *do, re, mi, fa-fa, mi, re, do.* The sounds ratched a dog's nerves, and he barked a vociferous and intermittent protest. The concierge ran out of his office inside a doorway and shouted to the owner of the dog, who replied in kind.

Caroline withdrew from the window. At any moment, someone in the uproar might call for partisans in his neighbours. A teasing aroma of coffee stole into the rooms, smells of garlic and tobacco, and warm spices used in flavouring cooking.

All these mixed with the exciting air of Paris, which was thin at this time of the year, but vibrant with life and exhilarating to those who loved this city as Caroline did.

A queer nostalgia tugged at Caroline's heartstrings.

Last night Caroline had decided that she must soon leave Paris. Today, in the light of the offer of this new job, that decision faded. If this new job were at all feasible she would stay.

The girls slept late in the morning and were awakened soon after eight o'clock by the shrill ringing of the telephone.

Fanny stretched out her hand and picked up the receiver. It was Georges, and she settled herself to listen to what he had to say. Caroline had wakened and was listening.

Then Fanny said: 'I'll pass it all on to Caroline and see what she says. Of course, she may turn it down." Fanny giggled. She seemed pleased with herself, and held a long telephone conversation. "Three o'clock sharp. Okay. Tonight still stands, of course. Aha… Aha!" She yawned luxuriously and said she was only half-awake. Then she said "Bye-bye," replaced the receiver and snuggled down between the sheets again, one eye looking at Caroline, who was leaning her cheek on her hand, her elbow propped up by the pillow, staring across at her.

"It was Georges, wasn't it?" asked Caroline.

"Yep! Are you good at figures, Caroline?" Fanny seemed wide awake.

"Not very. Why?"

"That's a bit of a setback. Men are so touchy where their pockets are concerned, and if it's a habit with you to count the cash wrong, then you are a washout."

Caroline did not reply, but she felt depressed. She might have guessed that this old M'sieur Pierre would make the job impossible.

"Are you tactful, a good mixer, and easy to get on with?" pursued Fanny.

"You should know." But the question made Caroline feel more hopeful.

"You may be tactful, easy on the eye and good-tempered, but I'll say you are below pass marks for being a good mixer," was the candid reply.

"I like people," said Caroline mildly.

"You like dogs, too," was the cryptic answer.

Caroline ignored this. "What else did Georges say?"

"Nothing much. To be frank, it was all terribly depressing. Just as I said, everything is still so much in the air. Raoul offers two square meals a day and pocket-money for long hours. It'll just about keep you in necessities in Paris, but you'll get no fun out of it. I'm sorry it is such a washout, honey. Of course, you can't accept such low terms. The man isn't human, but just a slave-driver."

"But what is the job?"

"I hardly care to tell you. It is as a kind of hostess in Raoul's exclusive restaurant which caters for a cosmopolitan clientele. He is of course known internationally. Also he would want you to keep an eye on the cash-desk or the cashier, I forget which, or it may be you keep both eyes on the cash itself. Anyway, it is not your kind of job." She paused, then said dramatically, "Oh, I am disappointed."

Caroline sank back on her pillow. A 'sort of job', a 'kind of hostess'. Then she recalled that Fanny was always vague. Things might not be so bad as Fanny thought. There would be no harm in finding out. She said calmly, deciding with the recklessness of desperation to take this job, "All the same, I shall go to see this M'sieur Pierre. I shall give his job a trial."

Fanny was quick to say, "It has not seriously been offered to you, so don't make a martyr of yourself in advance. That might well be waste of time."

Caroline frowned. She was not sure of Fanny this morning. Her behaviour was suspicious. "Then why did Georges ring you up at this unearthly hour?" she demanded.

"Goodness knows, unless he wanted to do his best for you and secure an appointment. Georges is always so kind-hearted."

"Then he wants me to see M'sieur Pierre?" said Caroline, her spirits rising.

"There can be no harm, I suppose. It may prove better than we think. If it is any good, there is bound to be a queue of girls lining up for it."

"When I shan't get a look in."

"I wonder. This man sounds horrible to me!" cried Fanny gloomily.

"I thought you knew him?"

"So I do," was the swift reply, "but I only know him from my side of the 'service'. I know nothing of his behaviour *behind* the scenes, where you will be."

"Where is this restaurant?" Caroline's voice was grim.

"Over on the left bank. You'll have to go by Metro. It is five minutes' walk from the station, facing the river, close to the bridge. Don't forget to allow for fares four times a day when you tot up the pay and how it has to stretch."

"Oh, of course," said Caroline, yet had Fanny not mentioned it, she would have forgotten that important point.

CHAPTER III

Punctually at nine o'clock that evening Caroline, in a simple black dress, with touches of white at the throat, and at the edges of the three-quarter sleeves, and wearing a light fur cape, and a small hat on her auburn hair, all part of Fanny's wardrobe, spoke to the big commissionaire, who, white-gloved, stood guard outside the glass revolving doors of the 'Maintenon'.

He bent his head to catch Caroline's request to see 'M'sieur Pierre'.

"Without an appointment that is not possible, ma'mselle," he said with a clipped Parisian accent.

"I have one at nine o'clock, m'sieur."

That of course was different, and the man's big curled moustache quivered as he looked more closely at this lovely girl, wondering why she was seeing M'sieur Pierre. It was always a matter of speculation to his staff as to who would eventually marry the boss.

Within minutes, Caroline was inside the 'Maintenon', her pale face bathed in the luminance of soft lights, her feet sinking deeply into the thick pile of a silver-grey carpet. She had a feeling of subdued elegance about her. Everywhere was a profusion of fresh spring flowers. Fanny had told her that to be inside the 'Maintenon' for the *first* time was like walking in a poem of beauty, of soft colours, and people speaking in muted voices, whose manners were polished and gentle. That was Fanny's extravagant way of expressing herself, but Caroline knew at once what she meant.

27

People in evening dress were in the foyer, and Caroline, as much for her unusual loveliness as for her formal day dress, was immediately an object of interest. She acted as a magnet to men. She was used to people looking at her, and took no notice of the admiration so eloquently expressed in dark approving eyes, but looked ahead of her.

Through a glass-panelled gilt-framed door Caroline caught a glimpse of the crowded restaurant. Waiters were moving about. Mink coats were thrown casually over gilt chairs. Jewels winked wickedly on women.

The head waiter, a magnificent figure in tails with a white tie, himself spoke to Caroline. He beckoned automatically to another lesser person in a dinner-jacket and black tie, who personally conducted Caroline to a small intimate lift, whose walls were panelled in peach quilted satin. Caroline approved of it all. *This*, she thought blissfully, *is a place of enchantment. It is like a scene from the Arabian Nights, or what I imagine it looks like.* This man was charming, a slave to do her bidding.

"This way, mademoiselle," the man said suavely.

Caroline stepped into the lift, and the man followed her. He closed the gilded door. They stood close together for the lift was only large enough for two, with a small tip-up seat upholstered like the panelling.

He spoke softly, not because he was a soft-spoken man, but because he could not help himself. It was a tribute to Caroline's flaming beauty, which fascinated him.

"M'sieur Pierre, does he expect you, Mees...?"

"May. Miss Caroline May."

The man repeated the name, giving them his own accent, so that they sounded to Caroline as strange as she was feeling.

The lift swung to a gentle stop. The man pressed a crystal button painted with a golden cypher of the lilies of France, and the door opened.

It was warm up here, for the central heating of the winter months had not yet been turned off.

The man stood back to allow Caroline to pass out, and again their arms touched. The man smiled self-consciously, but Caroline did not even notice him. Her mind had gone ahead, and she was wondering about this M'sieur Pierre, what he had to say to her, and how she should answer him, and more important than all, if she would suit him.

The man apologized, passed her in the narrow passage, and led the way towards a cream-painted door, where he knocked discreetly.

Caroline's heart beat fast. She had never applied for a job before, and had no experience of presenting herself to the best advantage. A queer thrill shot through her veins as a deep crisp voice, with the mellow intonation of an actor, called: "*Entrez!*"

The man opened the door with a flourish and said loudly, "Mees May, m'sieur," and stood back for Caroline to enter the room. She went forward slowly, wonderingly…

Raoul was waiting for Caroline. He was neither good nor bad-tempered, but highly critical. He had been annoyed with himself all day for allowing Georges, of whom, secretly, he had a poor opinion, to influence him: and he was sorry he had agreed, for the sake of peace from Georges, to meet this stranger. But Raoul had given his word, and he was not the kind of man to retract it. Indeed, he had gone to some pains to create a new post for this unknown girl whom Georges was determined to thrust upon him.

Raoul had decided to call her a 'Personnel Officer'.

This had been revealed at the weekly conference Raoul held with the heads of all departments, not only those concerned with the restaurant, but with the various small factories he ran as 'side-lines' to his principal business, and which were spread about in the environs of Paris.

The staff had not taken kindly to the idea at first. They were slow to accept an innovation, visualizing this new suggestion as a kind of superior welfare worker, with perhaps a social reform diploma to back her up. She might curtail their liberty and spy upon them.

Raoul had quickly dispelled the idea.

"She will be here more on the clients' behalf, than on yours," he told them. "When I add that she is a beautiful English girl, you will perhaps understand better."

They understood only too well.

To Raoul's astonishment they laughed readily, and winked knowingly at one another, exchanging witty jests in whispers, wondering if the boss had fallen in love at last.

Seeing this, and not understanding that he was the object of this wit, Raoul thought, *They will spoil her between them.* And he thought again, grimly, *I hope she is their idea of beauty or there will be trouble.*

At once they co-operated to make Caroline welcome and comfortable, and Raoul was compelled to remind them that she would be one of the paid staff and not an honoured guest as they appeared to think.

Raoul consulted the head waiter, Jean, as to where Miss May should eat.

It was a delicate point. Between them it was arranged that she should sit at a small table between the restaurant and the 'service', behind a bank of greenery and spring flowers, and a glass-panelled screen at her back.

"To shut out the draughts from the 'service', m'sieur," explained Jean. "The flowers will kill any smells that mademoiselle's nose finds offensive."

Everything was arranged before seeing Caroline, and that Raoul would do this evening. They were all a little excited about her coming. There was speculation and bets about her appearance.

Raoul had been down in the restaurant for a couple of hours, talking to patrons. He had kept an eye on his wristwatch, wondering if this girl would be punctual. Just before nine o'clock Raoul had come slowly up to his office, using the red-carpeted staircase in preference to the exotic little gilt lift.

Somewhere outside a clock was striking the hour.

I need not hurry, he told himself. *She is sure to be late. Fanny has no idea of time, and I suppose her friends are the same.*

He entered his office and closed the door, smiling vaguely at his secretary Nini, who from her desk in a far corner of his room looked across at him and smiled.

Raoul sat down at his desk.

Up to that moment he was cool and calm. Looking back at that moment Raoul knew that he was as sane as any man.

He was agreeably surprised to see the small red spot on his desk flicker, a sign from below that someone was on his way upstairs.

Subconsciously, Raoul straightened his black bow tie, and swept his hands back over his head. All seemed well.

Overcome by a sudden unaccountable shyness, Raoul picked up a pencil and began to make notes on his desk-pad.

He was acutely aware of sounds outside the room, the click of the lift gate as it was opened, and a moment later there was a second click as the gate was closed again.

Then came a knock at the door.

Raoul spoke more sharply than he was aware.

"*Entrez!*"

The door was opened, and Raoul saw Henri's familiar features.

"Mees May, m'sieur," said Henri, and though his face was purposely expressionless, there was a something in Henri's voice, a kind of trembling elation, which told Raoul clearly how the man regarded this girl.

I could make a guess that Miss May is the loveliest creature Henri has ever seen! crossed Raoul's mind.

Slowly Raoul shifted his gaze from Henri's blank face to the girl who had just come into the room.

In the long pause that followed, Raoul did not know it then, there passed one of the biggest moments of his life. He did not observe that Henri had withdrawn, closing the door after him.

Raoul's eyes met the large grey ones of Caroline May.

He got to his feet, and moved around the desk towards her. His movements were quick and eager. At sight of her, so radiant in her colourful loveliness, so poised, Raoul's blood stirred, and his heart was uplifted. He felt light-headed, too, and his mind, which was usually so disciplined and concise, did not seem so clear as usual. He smiled confusedly because it was difficult to look unmoved on such radiance, and he felt happy even to be privileged to gaze without seeming rude.

Caroline gave him no answering smile. She stood still, just within the door, her great questioning eyes fixed on Raoul, a queer disappointment tugging at her heart, because this man was *not* M'sieur Pierre. He did not fit in with the picture that Fanny had drawn of the owner of the 'Maintenon'. Something was wrong.

Far from being enamoured of his looks as Georges thought all women were, they only served to increase her fears that something she could not understand was working like an evil agency against her.

A sense of panic swept over Caroline. She turned swiftly towards the door, as though she would escape, but it was closed. She stood at bay, feeling trapped.

Raoul was close to her now. He held out his hand, smiling gently if a little fixedly, for it is difficult to retain the warmth of a grin in the face of a stony stare.

"Mademoiselle May?" Raoul came to a stop in front of her, clicking his heels together with precision. Then he said in English, "Good evening."

Caroline nodded slightly. "Good evening, m'sieur," she said in a faint voice.

Without realizing what she was doing, Caroline's hand went out to meet Raoul's.

"You are not M'sieur Pierre?" she asked suddenly in a hoarse tone.

Holding her fingers lightly in his, and raising her hand and bending his head in one movement, Raoul brushed the back of Caroline's hand with his lips; then raising his head, he dropped her hand and stood back a pace. The gesture was flowing and graceful, and over in a few seconds.

It was an impersonal greeting on Raoul's part. He had made it thousands of times in his life when meeting women, but there was a respect in the gesture which restored Caroline's confidence, and made her feel honoured and happy. It steadied her nerves just when every impulse within her was poised for flight.

"I am M'sieur Pierre, Miss May," replied Raoul with some amusement.

"Oh!" was all that Caroline could think of to say blankly.

Fanny was behind this meeting. Fanny had tricked her into coming, and Caroline was angry with herself for being duped so easily.

"Why are you so surprised when you look at me? Do I look so strange?" inquired Raoul, and Caroline was struck by the mellifluous, almost caressing note in his baritone voice.

It was not possible to tell this man that Fanny had described him as being old, fat, bald and a tyrant, so Caroline looked away from him, saying quietly, "*Pardon*, m'sieur."

As though he read her thoughts, Raoul said: "I am perhaps different from what you expected? Perhaps I should look old? As it happens, this evening I feel so middle-aged."

"Oh, no!" cried Caroline hurriedly.

"No matter," Raoul replied, seeing her embarrassment. "You are Miss May, and I am Raoul Pierre. This is my office. You have come here to discuss this work you wish to do for me. Shall we sit down?"

He spoke quietly, with an assurance in his voice that gave Caroline confidence. He turned to bring forward a chair, and in doing so was aware that his secretary from her little desk in the corner of the room was staring at him and his guest with interest.

With that Gallic swiftness of mind that belongs peculiarly to the French, with scarcely a pause Raoul said in a different voice: "But first of all, let me introduce my secretary-cashier, Mademoiselle Nini Dogas," and he waved his hand in the direction of the French girl, who rose and walked slowly across to them.

Caroline watched her approach. It was obvious that the girl was a personality. Her hair was black, the front curled into a 'bang' that cut like a knife across her white forehead, and seemed to emphasize her large, liquid black eyes. Her nose was thick and unremarkable, in that it probably went the way of all noses and suited her face. The compelling, stormy sultry eyes vied for notice with her wide mouth that was splashed like a vivid scarlet gash across her white face, just above the heart-shaped line of her jaw.

Caroline had seen girls like Nini in French films, ultrafeminine French girls, not beautiful but with unmistakable allure, and usually playing vampish parts. She wore a short, black skirt whose tightness restricted her movements. Her thin legs, encased in thin nylons, were perched on the top of the highest heels Caroline had ever seen. The sandal had a thick sole and nylon straps.

Nini, her eyes on Raoul, minced and tottered towards them, swaying her narrow hips slightly.

M'sieur Pierre smiled proudly at his secretary-cashier. It was obvious that he liked her.

As she came close to them, Nini's black eyes shifted to Caroline's face. Her expression was blank.

The girls bowed distantly to each other, then Nini spoke crisply and thinly in French, "*Bonjour*, Mademoiselle May."

Raoul smiled. There was nothing special in the meeting to make him smile, unless it was that curious emotion that had seized him the moment he set eyes on Caroline, and which had not yet died down. Suddenly, the depression of months had lifted, and he was happy and carefree as he had been as a young man doing military service and not burdened with the responsibilities of a career. He wanted to laugh and sing with sheer joy, and had to keep a tight hold on himself in case the laughter and singing should break out. None of this inner exuberance showed on his face except in that fatuous smile. Nobody guessed the will power he called up to keep his wild happiness within bounds.

He bridged over the awkward silence that fell upon the two girls after they had greeted each other by explaining in English, which was accented charmingly: "Nini is but another name for my — how you say it? — second-in-command. She knows all my business and most of its — ramifications, as well as I do — perhaps better. What the 'Maintenon' would do without Nini I do not know."

He spoke English fluently. Nini understood little of what Raoul said, so he explained in French. He had spoken with polite exaggeration, of course, but Nini was pleased. She adored compliments.

Caroline listened in silence, wondering if she took this post whether she would have to take orders from this second-in-command, who disliked her, as she would hate any girl who lived in close contact with M'sieur Pierre, at sight.

The girls made no pretence of having anything to say to each other now, and Nini shrugged eloquently and retired once more to the 'crow's nest' of her desk, and wished that the other two would talk in French instead of English, which she understood so little.

Raoul said once more, "Sit down, Miss May." He went back to his own chair on the other side of the big desk and, seating himself, looked across at this radiant stranger who had invaded his office looking for a job, and his heart — well, she would not know about that. At this early stage in their friendship she must not.

Raoul sat back easily in his chair, and began to question Caroline. In so doing he was able to feast his eyes on her unusual beauty without comment. It was a pleasant occupation. He forgot that he was a busy man, that he should be down in the restaurant, or hovering near it, ready for any sudden emergency, quick to settle the hundred and one small problems that occurred from time to time, because small problems soon grew tangled and difficult if not tackled at once. He felt relaxed, his heart beating fast, and his brain seething with all kinds of silly ideas.

"You know all about this job?" he asked, aware that he was the only person who did know about it, but he must say something business-like to show this girl, who was looking at him so warily, that he was serious.

Caroline shook her head. "Not much, M'sieur Pierre, except that it is a part-time job. My friend, Miss Cornell, was vague."

Raoul laughed a little. It was a pleasant mellow sound, indicative of a blithe spirit.

"She would be anyway. I know Fanny." He opened a drawer and took out a notebook, and flicked over a few leaves until he found the right page. "Now I shall tell you, for there must be no mistakes as to what you are letting yourself in for. Shall I read my ideas for you? Do not laugh even if they sound quaint to you."

"Please, M'sieur Pierre." There was no hint of a smile on Caroline's face.

Raoul read: "I shall require you to be on duty here each day from twelve until three o'clock, and again in the evening from seven until twelve. You will come half an hour before these times for your *déjeuner* and dinner, which you will eat in the restaurant.'" He paused with a look of annoyance, and glanced towards the telephone which was ringing insistently. "Nini!" he cried sharply over his shoulder, for she was slow to answer it.

Nini picked up a receiver.

"'Allo! 'Allo!" she called shrilly.

Raoul frowned, but determinedly shut out the sound of Nini's voice.

He continued reading his notes: "During those times you shall be seen by my clients in the restaurant, so that they may consult you if they wish. Remember, I want tact. My clients must have only the best. Even if you should think otherwise the client is always right, never wrong. Do you understand?"

"Ye-es," said Caroline doubtfully.

"You do not," Raoul remarked so abruptly that Caroline jumped. "If there is a grumble about food, if it is too hot or too cold, if the Chef fails to please or the service is not *par excellence* — if, *mon dieu*, there is one speck of smut on a plate, then you will report the fault to me at once. Sometimes a *nouveau riche* who cannot appreciate fine wines and good cooking finds his way here. He has heard of the 'Maintenon,' and wishes to boast to his friends at home that he has dined here. He may find fault with the *addition*. Our charges are high — but so are our costs. What would you? But call me. I shall settle such a man. Even you must call me if one lady — old, big and ugly — is by some misluck sitting in a bad light, one that is cruel to her age. It can be changed. She must be flattered into believing in herself. To be successful one must understand human nature. Do you not agree?"

Caroline nodded gravely. She was listening entranced, not so much because of these behind-the-scene revelations, but because it was such a joy to listen to this man's mellow voice. Even in anger Caroline was sure it could never sound harsh. In softness or when making love to a woman... Caroline flushed at her temerity. She must not think such thoughts. This was a business interview.

Raoul went on in his musical tones to which Caroline felt she could listen all day: "I have a large cosmopolitan clientele, and it is difficult to please everybody, yet that must be our aim. But that is not all your duty. When the restaurant is closed for the afternoon or the night, you will be responsible for taking the cash-box and putting it in the safe — over there," and Raoul nodded towards a large safe standing against the wall. "You will take it from Nini. It is something I usually do, but it often causes me inconvenience to be here when Nini has made up the accounts and wants the money put away in safety. I shall wish you to be here on Sunday. It is one of our busiest days."

Raoul glanced at the notebook, and went on diffidently: "For your services I shall pay you 3,500 francs a week. You will not be on the payroll of the staff, for then you must join the Union. If they should strike it would mean everyone in the restaurant might walk out on me at a moment's notice. I should not care for you to strike against me, Mademoiselle May. Your job as a personnel officer is in the nature of a try-out, and for the time being I shall pay you from my private purse. We will see how you get on. After one month we will talk it over again." Raoul paused. He closed the book and slipped it back into the drawer. "In your spare time," he told

Caroline deliberately, "and in mine, I should like you to read English with me."

Caroline was quiet for a long time. Thought was disconnected. It was the amount of the pay that seemed to overshadow in her mind what Raoul had said. The work was simple. She was to hold a 'watching brief', for the restaurant. She would have two meals a day. M'sieur Pierre spoke good English. Many men would be satisfied with such language achievement.

Then she said quickly, aware that he was looking at her, and waiting for her to speak, "You said it was a part-time job."

"So it is," he replied, puzzled.

"It is too much money for me. I have yet to prove myself."

Raoul liked her for that. Most people who came to him seeking jobs were more interested in the monetary worth of the work. But talking about money seemed to steady his quivering nerves, and he was able to think clearly on business lines.

"You know the value of 3,500 francs in sterling?" he asked.

"About three pounds ten shillings a week," Caroline replied after a pause.

"It is not much, believe me, Miss May. I admit I have not always had a good return for higher salaries than the one I am offering to you. I do not forget that midnight is a late hour for you to go home."

"I shall have two-thirds of the twenty-four hours for myself."

"Fifteen hours," corrected Raoul. He was fully recovered now. His voice was precise and business-like.

"You count the hour when I am eating work for you," she said, and the idea made her smile. Eating food in this wonderful restaurant could only be an honour and pleasure.

Raoul shrugged. He liked her fairness, even though it sounded unpractical to his business sense. He glanced sideways at Nini, who understood a little English and then only when it was spoken slowly. For once Raoul did not admire that business acumen which prompted Nini to demand 8,000 francs a week, plus her food, and fare to and from her home.

He also looked surreptitiously at his watch. Then he said: "Now I have explained clearly to you your side of the job, perhaps you would like to ask a few questions?"

His manner was crisp. Raoul knew he must soon go downstairs again, and be seen by his clients and his staff. There was an impatience in his manner to be gone. So far as he was concerned the interview was practically at an end. All that was required was this girl's 'yes'.

But while Raoul was speaking, Caroline had been turning the matter over in her mind, and looking at this new job from many angles.

She hesitated before speaking, aware that her acceptance of the job was hinged on the answer to her question. Then she said, "I was wondering what I would be expected to wear in the evening."

"I was waiting for you to ask me that. I see you have a sense of proportion. To mix with the clients who are invariably smartly dressed you would require a *décolleté* dress, quiet in colour, but if possible, a model gown. One would wish to make the correct impression."

There was a silence when Raoul had finished speaking.

Then Caroline said reflectively, "I see."

She was even now wearing a hat, dress and shoes which were cast-offs from Fanny's abundant wardrobe, and she wondered what evening dress Fanny could spare her to wear.

Caroline thought, *It is impossible for me to buy a dress.*

With quick perception Raoul understood her hesitancy, and said: "I do not expect you to buy a new dress for the job. The fact that you have come to me tonight, as someone seeking a job, is proof that you have not the money for an expensive dress."

Caroline flushed with humiliation. She was unused to discussing buying dresses with men.

But Raoul saw nothing untoward in the position. His manner was aloof. He might have been talking about the weather so impersonal was his tone.

He said: "The firm shall provide a suitable dress. I shall give you the name of a good house where they will take much pleasure in suiting you."

Caroline was still flushed, but anger had taken the place of her humiliation. This was going too far. What must he think of her to offer to buy clothes for her, a stranger to him?

"I should not dream of allowing you to do that," she said quickly.

There was that in her tone which annoyed Raoul. Silly little thing, she should be glad to hear that his business would provide suitable clothes for her. Obviously she could not appear in the evening in the wrong kind of dress. He raised his chin, and a look of hauteur seemed to change the expression of his face.

"*You* do not dream, Miss May!" he exclaimed. "*I* am not buying you a dress. I thought I had made it clear that the firm would do that. I do not care what you wear. I do not see you as a woman, but as an employee who must have a sense of discipline to make a success of her work. It is important for my business that everyone seen by the clients is dressed well. It is bad advertisement to appear in old-fashioned or shabby clothes. Please, we will say no more about it. You will order a dress from Toinette's without delay. Wait, you will weary people in the same dress, so order two or three."

It was the name of a famous dressmaker, and Caroline's eyes widened. Any girl would love to wear a dress designed by Toinette, but quickly Caroline knew it must not be.

She opened her mouth to speak, to refuse such a generous gift, even at the expense of the business. Fanny was sure to have something suitable that she would enjoy wearing. Then her eyes fell on Raoul's mouth. Hitherto the sensitive lips had been soft, sometimes smiling. Now his mouth was stern and set, and the dark eyes that met her inquiring gaze were proud and inscrutable.

M'sieur Pierre had made up his mind. He had spoken. Instinctively Caroline knew that she could not make him alter it.

Well, she had spirit, too.

She pushed back her chair and rose. "Thank you for being so kind as to see me, M'sieur Pierre. I will think over what you have said and let you know," she said. Try as she would Caroline could not keep the slight tremble from her voice.

Raoul heard it, and softened at once. He, too, had risen. They faced each other across the desk. Before seeing Caroline he had expected her to jump at anything he offered her, but since meeting her he knew she was not the kind to take a job without thinking it over. But once she had accepted she would do her best to stick to it. He dared not urge her to accept, yet in his heart Raoul had never wanted a thing so much in his life.

He said: "I think you will find you have plenty of time for your studies. You can follow art in the morning, before you come here. I know the lectures for languages at the Sorbonne take place in the late afternoon, for I have attended them myself for English lessons. I did not think to tell you that you have Monday in each week for yourself, and a weekend each month. It is not a bad job. Indeed, it could prove a good one. You are bound to make many contacts, any one of which may help you in the future. I could make it even easier for you, but that would not be fair to the rest of my staff, who would be quick to resent favouritism."

"That part is all right," Caroline admitted.

"Ah, then what is wrong?"

"Nothing."

"Why do you hesitate?"

"Well, I must think it over."

He thought, *Now she will have time to refuse.* "Is there anything to think over?"

"Oh, yes."

"I understood the matter was urgent."

"So it is."

"Then…"

Caroline said nothing. She was aware that M'sieur Pierre was standing there watching her closely, probably wondering why she did not rush to seize his generous offer of a play-time job. She thought, *Half an hour ago, before I had seen him, I would have done that.*

Caroline was aware of her reluctance to seize the chance. She chided herself for being so silly. Why be afraid of close contact with this man, of seeing him daily, talking to him? She should delight in serving him. Yet the fear was there.

It overshadowed everything. It grew with every moment she remained in that luxurious room — the fear of her own weakness. How fatally easy it would be to fall in love with this attractive man!

It could happen. Perhaps it had already happened, Caroline thought wildly. She thought, too: *I don't want to get involved with anyone. I want...* But quite what she wanted Caroline did not know.

"Are you not content with my proposition?" Raoul demanded. "Is it that you want more money?"

"Oh, no, please don't think that."

"Then you want more free time, perhaps?"

"No, I understand these are your business hours. It would be for me to fit in with them. It is only — well, I should like to talk it over with a friend first."

"Fanny?" snapped Raoul, and was relieved when Caroline agreed.

"Yes."

"She will tell you to take it."

"Perhaps." Caroline was still undecided. There was a long pause.

Then a curious thing happened. The telephone bell had been ringing on and off throughout the interview. It had constantly interrupted them. Nini had been answering it in her thin, shrill voice.

Then came a call which Nini could not answer. She teetered across the room and stood at Raoul's elbow waiting for him to notice her, with, for Caroline's benefit, a look of patient resignation on her face.

"What is it, Nini?"

Nini spoke in rapid French, "Madame la Marquise de la Fallière is on the telephone."

Raoul's expression changed miraculously. It was young and glad.

45

"*Pardon!*" He picked up a receiver from his desk, and his face was soft, smiling and expectant.

For one long agonizing moment Caroline felt as though someone had thrust a sword into her heart. The feeling was so great that she had an actual pain. Jealousy of the unknown woman seemed to freeze the blood in her veins. A confusion of thoughts rioted in her brain.

"'Allo, *chérie*," Raoul called softly. "Dar-r-r-ling! I am so glad to hear your voice. It shows that you are better." He spoke the last few words in English. His eyes dwelt on Caroline. Covering the mouthpiece for a moment with his hand he whispered, "My mother!"

Caroline looked down at the carpet. What a fool she had been! Somehow, she had not thought of this man with 'belongings'.

As he spoke in English obviously he did not mind her listening.

Suddenly, at the sound of his voice speaking in those loving and tender tones, everything was changed. A marvellous human being had emerged from the business man of the last half-hour. A fateful telephone call had given Caroline a chance of seeing the soul of a man. She forgot the fears that had beset her, fears which had taken shape when she realized that Fanny had made a fool of her, and this man might do the same. Caroline's mind, which had been confused, dithery and uncertain, was now made up. She would accept this post.

She felt an intruder, and bowing and smiling with the inner radiance of her thoughts, she made as though to leave the room.

Raoul saw the movement and put up his hand to stop her going.

Caroline nodded. She walked away and stood with her back to him, looking at a gay and colourful picture hanging on the plain grey wall. She saw nothing because she was thinking: *I will come at once. I will do as he wishes and buy a lovely dress at Toinette's. I am determined to make a success of my work so that he will be proud of me and glad that he has chosen me.*

Then she was aware that the talk had finished, the receiver was put back with a faint click, and Raoul was standing behind her.

She turned to face him and saw that his expression was tranquil. He was happy and contented. He said: "That was my mother. She has been so ill. I was worried about her for she is little and frail. I am so glad that she is better again."

"I am glad, too," Caroline replied, and she meant it.

Raoul preceded her to the door and opened it. He said, "Then I shall be hearing from you soon, Miss May?" He held out his hand and again he went through that charming gesture of bending to kiss her hand.

It was then that Caroline said bluntly, "When shall I begin work?"

He had not let go her hand and paused, still holding her fingers in his palm.

"You have decided, then?" He released her hand, but remained looking down at her.

"Yes."

"Then come tomorrow. If you get in touch with Toinette after ten o'clock tomorrow, you will find that I have already arranged for her to fix you up as soon as possible. Goodbye, Miss May."

"Goodbye, M'sieur Pierre."

Caroline turned away to find Henri waiting for her in the passage.

Raoul said, in French, "Will you please see mademoiselle to the door?"

The interview was over.

Caroline was aware of a sense of loss and coldness, yet the heating was still turned on and the building was warm. It remained with her as she followed Henri along the passage and shared the lift with him, a feeling only bearable when she thought, *I shall see him tomorrow.*

Henri smiled at her, his alert eyes looking at her in a warm interesting way which at any other time would have made Caroline feel faintly resentful, but which now she did not notice.

She was aware of the luxury of the lift which was small and intimate, like a lady's boudoir, and she thought: *How lovely to work here and to be able to use this lift, and to see beautifully dressed people and eat well-cooked food. How lucky I am!*

As the lift reached the ground floor and the door was opened, there was a sudden sound of gaiety and life, the convivial noise, like the hum of many bees, of people enjoying themselves, the many threads of cross-talk resulting in a pleasant hum.

The restaurant was apparently full to capacity, for the magnificent flower-decorated foyer was crowded with people jostling one another and talking many different languages.

The atmosphere was heavy and redolent with the mingled fragrance of exotic perfumes and cigars.

Henri accompanied Caroline to the revolving doors to the street. He bowed her out, and turned back quickly to plunge into the crowd waiting restlessly for attention and direction. The excitement in the air stirred Caroline's pulse.

She was aware, too, that at this moment, she herself was in no better shape than these people, and must get herself sorted out. She was still emotionally disturbed through meeting M'sieur Pierre, and happy, too, in an unreasoning way, because M'sieur Pierre had said nothing that could cause such happiness. His manner had been business-like throughout the interview. He had been cold, distant, impersonal — even impatient at her slowness in accepting his point of view; but somehow she had sensed a friendliness behind the aloof facade, had caught a warm gleam in the brown eyes that searched her face intently as though probing for the truth. Then, at the last, she had glimpsed a warmth, affection and love in him — not for her, of course, but for his mother. It showed him in a new light, and she had been swept off her feet with longing that she might have the chance of making him some day feel that way about her. In the light of reason Caroline knew how impossible this was. But somehow her dreams dimmed that light of reason.

Caroline told herself that M'sieur Pierre had been unexpected, so unlike her ideas of a restaurant-keeper. He was young, handsome and tall as Caroline liked her dream man to be. He had charming manners, and behaved more like an actor than a business man. Yet there was not the picture of an actor in him, but something solid and worthwhile, otherwise how could he have won through to success?

So engrossed was Caroline in her thoughts that she missed the long line of marvellous cars that were drawn up outside the 'Maintenon', in a sleek, gleaming line alongside the kerb, any one of which would have won a prize in a *Concours d'Élégance*. All the way across Paris in the Metro, Caroline was thinking: *This is fantastic. I do believe I have done what I have laughed at Fanny for doing. I have fallen in love.*

It was silly, of course, and hopeless, but oh, how lovely it was to dream, and to wish that the dream would come true!

Caroline lingered in the cobblestoned courtyard off the rue Tino. She was shy of meeting Fanny, whose quick eyes spotted everything that was going on about her, inside and outside a person. Caroline longed to talk things over with her friend, for though Fanny was always gay and seemingly superficial and flighty-minded, there was an inner core, seldom touched it was true, which hid the nicest and truest part of herself.

Looking up at the room, Caroline saw that the window was in darkness. Fanny was out with Georges, her evening only just begun.

There would be time to get into bed before Fanny came back. If she were too shy to talk about M'sieur Pierre, it would be easy to pretend to be asleep.

CHAPTER IV

Caroline was in bed, lying awake in the darkness, when Fanny came home. It was after midnight, and the City, though still bathed in golden light, was quieter.

Fanny switched on the light, but Caroline remained for a while with closed eyes, though the light hurt her eyes under the heavy lids, and she longed to open them.

Then Caroline realized that Fanny had come close to her. She was standing by her bed, looking down at her.

Unable to keep her eyelids still, and knowing the pretence of being asleep to be thin, Caroline opened her eyes and said: "Hello, Fanny!"

"I was wondering when you were going to wake up and tell me all about it," said Fanny with a laugh. "Well? Are you too tired to talk?"

"No, I want to. I've got the job."

"Of course," Fanny replied easily. Then she inquired, "How do you like Raoul?"

The question seemed to satisfy some inner hunger with Caroline, and she brightened at once, though she was still shy about discussing Raoul.

"Very much," she forced herself to say. Then she added, "Why did you tell me he was old?" But the question did not seem important this morning. It did not matter.

"Because, honey, you had the jitters. If you had known that Raoul is the handsomest man in Paris with the looks of a film star, the manners of a diplomat, and what it takes to put his personality over, you would not have gone to see him. I didn't dare upset your picture of what a restaurant-keeper looks like.

You must admit I acted well in the best way. I wanted so much for you to meet Raoul. So did Georges."

"You seem to know him quite well," Caroline said, and wondered: *Why should Fanny have made such a "thing" of my seeing M'sieur Raoul? Why should she and Georges have plotted for me to do so?*

Caroline did not really care how well Fanny knew Raoul, but now the subject was opened, she wanted to talk about him. It made her feel cosy and warm and important to know him.

"Of course I know him, but not privately, though I know he visits my aunt occasionally on a Sunday, when she holds a *salon* to meet well-known people. I have heard that in his private life Raoul is — exclusive. Georges says he is a bit of a mystery to the Press."

"What do you mean?"

"Oh, nothing derogatory. I have told you that Raoul is a self-made man with a background of the old *régime*. Blue blood does not always work out well, but he seems to have done the trick. He is a good republican now. Anyhow, I should not have suggested your seeing him if Raoul were not perfectly straight."

"Why ever not? I can take care of myself."

Fanny giggled, then she mocked: "They say that the Lord looks after children and drunks. Though you may be brainy, honey, you are a baby in experience of the world, and with men like Raoul, who have knocked about life; or can it be that life, as I know it, passes over you without touching you? Some girls seem to be born with a perpetual 'youngness', and even when they grow old never quite lose it." She watched Caroline's innocent eyes while saying this. They were wide open and clear. Fanny laughed shortly and said impatiently, "It is like talking to a sleeping child to make you see what I mean."

Caroline did not reply. She had turned her head a little and was staring at the ceiling, and Fanny thought, *I wonder if I have started something there.*

She said boldly, "I believe you have fallen for Raoul, haven't you?"

"That would be quick work," Caroline remarked quietly, dreamily — evasively. "I hardly know him."

Fanny's face took on a hopeless expression. "Falling in love *is* quick work. One moment you are not in love, and the next you are."

"Is that how it is with you?" Caroline inquired.

Fanny laughed. She was not deceived by Caroline's guile. "Now perhaps you'll understand what is meant by love at first sight."

"Oh, I wouldn't call *that* kind of fancy love," said Caroline quickly. But the disparagement was meant to hoodwink Fanny, for that was exactly what must have happened to her last night.

Fanny had hit the mark and knew it. The signs were not new, and she read Caroline's mind like a book. "Time will show, honey. You are too smart-looking for art and languages to take more than a small span out of your life. There's more in it than those. You'll soon learn that love is necessary to a girl. It gives her bloom. And shall I laugh?"

Caroline smiled. She was feeling excited and foolish, and laughter came easily this morning. "You seem to be taking a great interest in my emotional life."

"I guess it's because I'm sick of seeing you so serious. Not to want to be loved, or to have the need of some emotion, is wrong. It is a woman's first step to failure. I hate failures. Besides, it's catching."

"You like parading emotions, and I don't. You talk about love too much to feel deeply."

"Maybe you are right."

Caroline did not want to be like Fanny who fell in and out of love so easily. The recovery after an *affaire* was a painful process, of bitter-sweet memories that sometimes brought regret and tears, and were inclined to harden Fanny's character. Usually they were both upset for days — until a new friend came along for Fanny.

Caroline looked affectionately at Fanny. It was queer how mixed her own emotions were this morning. One moment she was glad to be in love, then she denied it because she was afraid, and again Caroline was sorry for herself.

They talked about clothes, and Fanny generously offered the loan of her wardrobe.

Even in her sleep, when the turmoil of her thoughts permitted sleep, Caroline saw Raoul, remembering the sensitive but chiselled mouth and the obstinate line of his jaw.

CHAPTER V

Next morning, soon after ten o'clock, Caroline telephoned Toinette's. The big dressmaking establishment was in a fashionable quarter of Paris, and she felt some temerity in speaking to them. Toinette's was a world-famous firm. Any one of her dresses was beyond Caroline's purse. She did not like approaching them. But she was told that M'sieur Pierre had already been in touch with them and explained his requirements. She was asked to call at her convenience.

Caroline decided to miss her art class and visit the dressmaker's *salon* at once, before her courage to face them ebbed when she might find it impossible to carry out M'sieur Pierre's orders. She was well aware of the shortcomings of her wardrobe, and did not look forward to submitting herself to their critical gaze. Caroline wished she could have taken the job without having to suffer the ordeal of being fitted for suitable clothes, dresses beyond her purse and which she could never afford to buy, but which she must have to wear as a part of her job. M'sieur Pierre had been adamant, and reluctantly Caroline had to agree that there was something in his point of view. Fanny had some lovely clothes, but nothing created by such a notable house as Toinette's.

The ordeal was nothing like as trying as Caroline had expected. To her surprise Caroline discovered quickly that the dressmaker and her assistants were human, and anxious to show as many people as possible what they could do. They knew all about her new job, and were keen for their own sakes to make her look her best. They looked upon her as a good advertisement for them. They took a delight in fitting her slim and lovely figure, and worked hard for an hour to please her. They chose three evening dresses for her, all models that had been worn by their own mannequins at dress shows, in which Caroline looked ravishing and which they thought Caroline would feel pleasure in wearing. They said the dresses would be packed at once and sent to the 'Maintenon' for M'sieur Pierre's approval.

Caroline was forced to agree, though she did not like the idea of M'sieur Pierre opening the box and looking at her dresses. Then she sighed, realizing that the dresses could never be hers for they belonged to the 'Maintenon'.

Caroline had no intention of going to the 'Maintenon' and reporting for duty before twelve on her first day. She returned to her room off the rue Tino for some black evening shoes and packed them in a small case together with some toilet accessories.

She was glad that Fanny was out, or she would have been chivvied off to work, and that would have restarted the argument which the two girls had begun last night as to what time she should report for duty.

When discussing this point with Fanny last night, Caroline had positively refused to take on her duties at eleven-thirty, in time to accept hospitality from the 'Maintenon'.

"Nonsense, go and eat a good meal. It is there or you would not be asked to eat it. Raoul expects it. There will be no time to eat until after three, and you will be ravenous."

"I don't care. It wouldn't be fair, just plain greedy."

"Silly, that is being quixotic, idiotic and romantic. You will start off on the wrong foot if you annoy him by not reporting to time."

"I shall be in time."

"Not to eat."

"Well, not today. Tomorrow will be different."

"You seem to want to make a good impression on someone," Fanny remarked drily.

"I want to make a success of the job."

"By going hungry to work."

"There won't be time to feel hungry. It will all be too new."

"Okay, but don't blame me if Raoul puts you on the carpet. And don't cry if you don't like what he says."

"I certainly won't shed tears on M'sieur Pierre's account. I can promise you that."

"Oh, sure!" agreed Fanny amiably, but she lifted her eyes for inspiration and help to the ceiling.

Caroline did not hurry to the Metro, but sauntered along, gazing into shop windows, not seeing the goods displayed because her mind was on M'sieur Pierre.

And so, deliberately, in a leisurely manner, Caroline went to the 'Maintenon', where the first of these small matters of etiquette to which Caroline had not given a thought, and of whose existence she was ignorant, cropped up.

She arrived at the restaurant at a moment when Maurice, the tall and dignified doorkeeper, chosen because of his massive and impressive figure, was shepherding a great lady through the revolving glass doors.

Caroline slipped aside to let the lady, and her escort, a young man, pass.

The lady acknowledged the polite gesture with a regal inclination of her head, but her escort hesitated, waiting for Caroline to precede him.

Caroline moved, and would have gone in. It seemed a natural thing for her to do. Then suddenly, steely fingers on her arm made Caroline pause. Under the pressure of Maurice's ungentle hand, Caroline even took a step backwards. In doing so she trod inadvertently on Maurice's highly polished boot. He appeared to wince, looked at her with sudden hatred, but said nothing.

His hand slipped away from her arm.

The great lady and her escort went into the 'Maintenon', and were already being received by Henri.

Caroline stood outside the door which had stopped revolving. She turned to look up at Maurice, whose massive figure towered above her like an avenging spirit.

Maurice spoke. It sounded more like a hiss than a voice, for the words came from between his teeth. "Ma'mselle is on the staff. She must use the staff entrance. It is at the back."

Caroline flushed at her mistake. She said something about being sorry and fled away from the important front entrance and hurried round to the back. She passed dustbins filled with garbage and met lorries delivering crates of goods. The passage was grey and drab. Over a door was the sign 'Maintenon'.

Inside the open door, seated within a small office, where he could check ingoing and outgoing traffic, was an old man.

Caroline spoke to him gently, realizing that she must keep a lookout for snags by being as friendly as possible with everyone on the staff.

By now Caroline was feeling a little unnerved. Quite how she had expected to be received she did not know, but it was not like this.

She walked quickly along the stone passage and through another door, and found a lift. She asked the liftman, who was busy cleaning his teeth with a horn toothpick while waiting for passengers, to take her up to M'sieur Pierre's office. She spoke with the authority of desperation, and it answered, for the man slipped his toothpick into a small inner pocket of his jacket, beckoned her to step inside the lift, slammed the door with a resounding crash, and took her swiftly upstairs.

There was no need for Caroline to ask the way along the thickly carpeted top passage. There was but one way to go.

Here she met a man who did not seem to be in the hurry that governed everyone's movements down below. He was young and pleasant-looking, and ready to be friendly and smile at Caroline, so that some of the warmth which Maurice's chilly reception had driven from her heart came back again in a flood.

They both hesitated by a window through which could be seen a medley of old roof tops and all kinds of chimneys; and sideways, between the roofs, there was a glimpse of the River Seine and the twin squat dark towers of Notre Dame Cathedral.

On impulse, the young man cried pleasantly in English, "Hello, what are you doing here?"

It was delightfully surprising to be spoken to in English. Caroline would have guessed his nationality anyway if she had not been so flustered. This blond, blue-eyed man wearing English-cut clothes could not possibly be mistaken for anyone but English, and a queer nostalgia for England and home swept over her so that she yearned to see her people again, if only for a short while.

She said: "I am new here and feeling rather at sea. I am making such stupid mistakes, and everyone appears too busy to bother about me and put me right."

"Lunch-time is both a busy and a serious occupation here," the young man told her with a grin. "I haven't the faintest notion what to do for you, but I shall be only too happy to be of any assistance to you."

"M'sieur Pierre engaged me yesterday. I sort of belong here now."

"Oh, you do! Unfortunately, I am not on the staff." A note of regret crept into the man's deep voice as he gazed with open admiration at the lovely face before him. "I wish I were. What exactly is your job?"

The fact that they were both English, and in a foreign country, created a bond of friendship between them, and Caroline's spirits rose mercurially. She forgot to long for home. Here was a bit of England standing over six feet tall in front of her.

"I am the new personnel officer to the restaurant," she told him laughingly as though she were making a joke. Indeed, it did sound like a joke to her just then.

"What is that? It seems to me as though old Raoul has created a post for one of his girlfriends. If that is the case you are going to enjoy yourself taking a nice fat pay-packet with practically nothing to do but look pretty. Beauty certainly has some sweet rewards," said the blithe young man, putting two and two together with alarming speed.

Caroline's face clouded. *So that is what people are going to think of me,* she thought, and all her fears and suspicions returned against Raoul in strength, so that his presence was handsome and benign no longer, but took on the aspect of a malign monster.

But it hurt in some strange way, too, that this man should speak so disrespectfully of Raoul, as though he thought him frivolous, putting his love affairs before his business. Even

Fanny, remembered Caroline with clarity, had called M'sieur Pierre a man of experience.

Caroline looked so serious and troubled suddenly that the man, who was watching the lights and shadows of expression flitting across her face, said quickly in an apologetic tone: "Perhaps I should not have said that?"

"You should not. But it is of no matter. I am not one of M'sieur Pierre's friends, but an employee in the firm."

The man appeared astonished. He looked more closely at Caroline's face, noting the glorious colour of her hair, the unusual combination of grey eyes with auburn hair, and the clear delicacy of her skin, and he thought in sudden perplexity: *What's going on here? If she isn't Raoul's Number One special now she soon will be. A man must be blind not to fall for this girl. A fastidious fellow like Raoul knows by instinct how to pick 'em.*

"I have a part-time job here, and…" Caroline explained at length what a personnel officer at the 'Maintenon' would have to do.

The young man pursed his mouth into a silent whistle.

"I shouldn't have thought such a person was necessary in a well-run restaurant like this," was all he could think to say.

"It must be if M'sieur Pierre thinks so."

"Then of course it is," the man agreed with suspicious politeness. "I have learned never to question what M'sieur Pierre does. He seems to rule this place like a despot. But I can't help my thoughts. Thank heavens he can't control those, or I have no doubt he would. I can tell you in confidence that it sounds odd to me. There is, of course, no comparison between us. I am only an ordinary fellow, while he is known to be a demon for perfection of detail. It is like him to think up an extra cog for a wheel. To be frank, as I study his books, I am often struck by the wealth of detail and the money that goes into it."

He was clearly puzzled and unconvinced, and continued to gaze at Caroline as though fascinated by her, much to her embarrassment.

Then Caroline demanded, "Who are you?"

"That is an easy one," was the modest reply. "I am the English member of a firm of accountants who examines the books of the 'Maintenon' periodically. I come here every quarter, and my work takes a week. I have spent the morning with Nini Dogas. She is a character, I can tell you. She oozes French femininity. You have probably met her, I don't suppose you will see her through my eyes. But she has her uses here. She knows everything that goes on in this establishment, and what she doesn't know she will find out — if it is worth knowing. She will put you wise to anything that puzzles you." The man glanced at his wristwatch. "I should be eating my lunch now instead of talking to you."

"Are you lunching downstairs?"

"With the mink coats? Oh, no. I can't run to the prices they ask here. I go around the corner, to a little restaurant where the food is good and not too expensive. Anyway, Madame knows me as a regular, and so I get a bit off the bill, and sometimes an extra titbit on my plate. What's your name?"

"May. Caroline May."

"May what?"

"Just May. It is my surname."

"Oh!" There was a short silence while the young man rolled Caroline's name over his tongue. Then he said: "You've shown no curiosity about my name, but I am going to tell it just the same, for I have a hunch we are going to see a great deal of each other in the future. It's Kit Dale. Call me Kit. You'll be doing it before the week is out, so why not save time by beginning now?"

He took a pace nearer to Caroline as though to compel her attention.

They stood looking at each other.

A door was opened at the end of the corridor and Raoul came out. He was looking for Caroline. She had not turned up and he was getting anxious.

Raoul had been up and down between his office and the restaurant several times. He made inquiries but no one had seen Mademoiselle May.

Raoul had just made up his mind that Caroline had changed her mind again, and was not coming. He decided to go down to the restaurant and forget her.

That was easier to say than do, for try as he would Raoul was already finding that Caroline was an unforgettable person. Raoul tried with all his will to push her from his mind, yet her image remained constantly before him. Then he saw her, standing in his corridor, talking intimately to one of the accountants. Dale was looking at her hungrily as though he found her delectable.

A flame of jealousy such as Raoul had never known shot through his veins. His anger rose against both of them. He felt hot and cold with fierce emotion. This was intolerable.

He saw them a moment before they were aware of him. It was long enough for Raoul to see that Dale was looking down at her, a special expression on his face. It made a deep-rooted impression on Raoul. He noted the lazy eyelids, and the soft luminosity in the light blue eyes. It was the drooping but inviting look of the born flirt, of a man who is ready and willing at all times to play at being in love with a beautiful girl because she expects it and he wants it.

Ordinarily Raoul would have observed all this and smiled indulgently, but not now, where this girl was concerned. He was angry now because, deep-rooted within him, Raoul had hall-marked this special girl for his own. He would have liked to put her under a glass case, and surround her with red cord as they do the exhibits in museums, only that of course was impossible. As he was forced to stand by and say nothing, his anger mounted until he was staring at them through a red mist. It was all he could do to stop himself from rushing forward and pushing them apart. But a shred of common sense told him that if he did anything so silly and drastic in these early stages of acquaintanceship he would lose Caroline for ever.

It made matters worse because Caroline seemed to like this man. *Why not?* he thought fiercely. *Dale is one of her countrymen, an attractive man who is ready for a bit of fun.* And he thought, too: *How dare the fellow monopolize her when she should be working for me? I engaged her. She is mine.*

Quickly Raoul conquered his emotions, and stifled his riotous thoughts. It was a great effort. It left him trembling.

He strode forward, his hands clenched to hide their shaking.

They heard him and turned their heads towards him.

Kit's smile grew fixed, and Caroline's faded away. Her face was serious as she waited for Raoul to join them, but her heart beat fast and painfully at his nearness, and she thought wildly, *How on earth am I going to hide my feelings for him?* Seeing Raoul in the flesh reminded Caroline why she was in this building, something she had momentarily forgotten.

"Good morning, Miss May," Raoul snapped.

"Good morning, M'sieur Pierre," she replied, startled by the rasp in his lovely baritone voice. She thought he was cross because she was late, and ventured to say, "I am sorry, I am afraid it is after twelve."

Then she remembered that their positions were changed since yesterday. Then he had been a kind of suppliant, begging her to join him. Today he was her boss.

Both of them forgot Kit Dale, who was looking from one to the other, his face expressive of puzzled wonder.

Raoul glanced significantly at his wristwatch. He had been so worried about her lateness. Either she had changed her mind and decided against coming, or there had been an accident. Yet nothing untoward had happened. She was here all the time, calmly enjoying herself with his accountant.

He said coldly, "*You are late.*" It sounded an unforgivable accusation.

Caroline did not reply. She was suddenly unhappy and wretched because M'sieur Pierre was displeased with her.

Raoul went on speaking. "Perhaps you will kindly go to my office, and wait for me there, when I will tell you what to do. I have an appointment now but it will not take long."

There was a pause.

For one moment, Caroline rebelled. She was unused to being spoken to in that distant tone, and resented it because Raoul used it before Kit Dale. The latter was looking at her with a mocking light in his blue eyes. There was a quirk to his mouth which told Caroline plainly, in the fleeting glance she gave him, that he was secretly laughing at her.

Then she remembered that it was her own fault she was late, that Raoul Pierre was right to speak to her for unpunctuality. Supposing everyone in the 'Maintenon' decided to be late? What then? It would spell failure and have to close down.

He was right and she must take the rap. *Oh, dear, what a beginning!* Caroline thought.

Kit spoke hurriedly. "I must be getting along, too, or I shall find the best things are 'off'." Then he smiled reassuringly at Caroline, who was looking downcast. "See you later, perhaps."

Caroline nodded. She felt too miserable to say anything.

Raoul had listened grimly. He thought, *Perhaps.*

He stood there while Caroline went in one direction and Kit in the other. He did not move until the door of his office was closed, and the lift gate was shut.

Then he stood by the open window looking down at the scene Caroline must have observed, the irregular roofs, and the assortment of chimneys, and the grey river sideways and beyond. He thought: *I must keep her so busy on my affairs. I shall have my eye on her, for if I do not he shall steal her from me before she is aware that she belongs to me.*

CHAPTER VI

Caroline, with mixed feelings, her head held high, went into the office. She expected to see Nini Dogas, who Kit had just assured her missed nothing. She was pleasantly surprised to find that Nini was not there. It occurred to Caroline that Nini had gone to lunch. She hoped that the French girl would stay away until everything was peacefully settled between M'sieur Pierre and herself.

Caroline was afraid suddenly lest M'sieur Pierre should find she was not after all suitable for his work, and tell her to go, and the happiness that had seemed to wrap about her like a rich cloak all day fell away so that she shivered as with cold and loneliness. Then, when she was feeling so depressed, her eyes fell on three dress boxes that were stacked up near the door, and which she had not noticed when entering the room. Toinette's name was splashed across them in scarlet lettering. They had not been opened, for the silken cord which was wound extravagantly about each box was still tied with the expert fingers of the showroom woman. A thin thread of pleasure cheered Caroline's wretchedness, like a coloured wool enlivens a drab pattern of tapestry. The boxes were addressed to 'M'sieur Pierre'. They were his property.

Caroline, still holding her attaché-case, waited in a growing fever of impatience for a long while, or her longing to see Raoul made it seem so. She glanced at his desk, finding interest in his writing-pad, the top page covered in notes written by him — a clear, straightforward writing with no flourishes or conceit in it. There were his pen and pencil, and a half-smoked cigarette on an onyx ashtray decorated with a couple of bronze hounds. And with its back to her, stood a photograph. Caroline wondered whose photograph it was that watched him write and telephone, and kept him mute company all the while he sat at his desk. Curiosity made Caroline rise from her seat. She must see the face of that photograph. Just as she was about to move there was a sound outside the room.

Caroline sank back quietly, a guilty flush rising to her cheeks. She had been trying to spy on him! A moment later Raoul entered the room and closed the door with a decided click.

Caroline knew who it was. She did not turn to greet him but waited until he moved across the room and sat down in his desk-chair facing her.

"Well?" he asked quizzically, and by his voice, sweet, low-toned and mellow, as when she had first heard it, Caroline knew that Raoul's anger was dead.

She spoke, saying the first words that occurred to her, because out there in the passage, with Kit listening and looking, she had felt that her apology was not adequate. She was desperately sorry, not for being late, but for causing Raoul to be angry.

"I am sorry I was late, M'sieur Pierre. It shall not happen again," she said earnestly, and the lovely grey eyes that met those quizzing brown ones were soft with entreaty, so that Raoul felt an overpowering desire to comfort and forgive.

Raoul wanted to smile. He longed to say soft things, to whisper that nothing mattered now because she was here, that to see her sitting there so quietly was worth the tortuous time of doubt and waiting. But the agony of that hour, when he had thought her lost to him for ever, was not to be endured twice. His feelings were strong, but his will was stronger and he said calmly instead, "You were exactly three quarters of an hour late, Miss May." His voice was devoid of expression.

"Oh, no, M'sieur Pierre," Caroline replied with spirit. "You are mistaken; I was only fifteen minutes late."

Raoul frowned. "Your time here is eleven-thirty o'clock."

"Surely only if I am here for *déjeuner*?" she asked in surprise.

"Why were you not here?" Then he added: "Put down that case. There is no point in keeping it on your lap like a baby, or as if you are about to run off in a hurry."

"I — was not hungry." Caroline smiled a little because his words assured her that he would not be sending her away.

"But you must be hungry, or you will be by three o'clock. There will be no time for you to eat when you wish. It is as I order. The client can choose his hour to eat, but not an employee in my restaurant."

"I understand, m'sieur."

"You may: but how do you expect to work well if you have not eaten since your *petit déjeuner*! What time did you have that, Miss May?"

"About eight-thirty, m'sieur."

"What did you have?" Raoul began to question remorselessly.

"A cup of coffee and a croissant."

"With butter?"

"Oh, no."

"Does Fanny eat butter?"

"Of course."

"Then why do not you?"

"Because — I cannot afford it."

"You could share Fanny's. I am sure she would be willing to do so."

"Yes, that is like Fanny. She would share everything she has."

"Then what stops you?"

Caroline reared her head proudly, then she hesitated. "Because…" she began, but could not go on.

"Ah, you are independent. That is what I thought. Now you are being absurd, showing a pride that is false. You owe it to your work, and to me, to eat properly. In future you will be here at eleven-thirty. It is my order. I have a reputation to keep up with my staff. I should not like it to be a failure because of one silly girl."

"Yes, M'sieur Pierre."

Then Raoul said, "*Bien*" and closed his lips with a snap.

The telephone rang and Raoul answered it, talking to someone for several minutes. When he had finished, he made some notes, and crossing to Nini's desk he tossed the page on to it.

When he returned, Raoul spoke to Caroline in a kinder tone. "As I said, I telephoned to Toinette and told her to show you some suitable dresses. Later she rang through to say you had chosen some." He glanced at the boxes by the door. "There are the boxes of dresses. You will please wear one of them tonight. There is a *boudoir* set apart for the women on my staff, so that you can change here. Mademoiselle Dogas will give you a key for a spare locker so that you may leave your hat and bag in safety. Is it understood?"

"Thank you, M'sieur Pierre."

The intercom telephone buzzed, and Raoul answered it. "I will come at once," he said in French, then replaced the mouthpiece carefully, but seemed in no hurry to go.

Caroline asked anxiously, "Did Madame tell you the cost of the dresses, M'sieur Pierre?"

"*Certainement.* That is business. Why do you ask?"

"Because they are expensive. I hope you weren't shocked at the price."

A look of annoyance crossed M'sieur Pierre's face, and Caroline was aware that she had offended him again, and thought miserably, *I always seem to start off on the wrong foot.*

Raoul said coldly: "When I want your opinion, Miss May, I shall ask for it. But since you have done so, if I have any fault to find with your choice it is that they are not dear enough. Cheap clothes are a waste of francs. I do not grudge a sou spent to perfect my business, while the members of my Board think as I do. Also, had I thought you should be extravagant according to my standards, or ready to choose dresses because of their cost rather than their good cut and line, I should not have permitted you to get them without my supervision. But from the opinion I had formed of you at our last interview I knew you could be trusted to buy something good, so that while following my ideas of a 'quiet' dress, I thought you would find something beautiful as well."

Caroline looked pleased at this compliment. She was not sure whether M'sieur Pierre meant to compliment her. She thought he was enjoying airing his English, for he liked using longer words than necessary, and was evidently proud of the fluency with which he spoke.

"Would you like to see them?" she asked.

He raised his hands as though shocked.

"No, that will be my pleasure when you wear them." Then the buzzer of the house-phone went again, and Raoul rose with a sigh. "Now please go to the boudoir and take off your coat, not your hat. I will wait to take you downstairs, and show you what I wish you to do."

They went out of the office, and M'sieur Pierre directed Caroline to a room labelled 'Boudoir'. She did not wait to look about her, but slipped off her coat and hung it up on a free peg, only waiting to glance at herself in a large mirror to see if her face was presentable, before rejoining Raoul.

He was waiting for her, and as she saw him Caroline loved him afresh, not because he was a fine, handsome figure of a man, but because she had just recalled how kindly and softly he had spoken to his mother on the telephone last night.

Raoul looked gravely at Caroline as she approached him. He was a busy man. There were people waiting to see him to whom time spelled money, yet he kept them waiting because this girl who had come so suddenly and fantastically into his life, 'out of the blue', fascinated him. The comprehensive glance which he gave to Caroline as she approached seemed to linger over every detail in her make-up.

He said nothing, and Caroline did not know whether he was pleased with her or otherwise, for he turned away suddenly.

For the first time he showed signs of hurrying, and did not wait for the lift, but went through a door leading to a quiet little-used staircase, and ran swiftly downstairs, down and around, over the red carpet, with Caroline at his heels.

In the foyer they were met by Henri, who looked at Caroline with reproach.

"M'sieur —" he began, but Raoul waved him aside.

"Presently, not now, Henri. Can you not see that I am busy?"

"But, m'sieur —"

"Let it wait."

Caroline heard the familiar hum of many people talking. Looking into the softly lighted restaurant she caught glimpses of mink coats flung casually over the backs of gilt chairs, the mingled fragrance of many scents, of food and wines, perfumes and cigars. It was impossible to pick out one smell. What made a smell seem like an exotic scent was the aroma of the whole place. There were flowers everywhere, with mimosa and lilac from the south of France predominating — the fluffy yellow balls of the mimosa mixing freshly with the twin blooms of white lilac. Waiters were hurrying to and fro, their movements practised and quiet, their little white-jacketed *commis* scuttling quietly about like little white mice.

M'sieur Pierre turned to her. His dark eyes met hers confidently. "You will follow me," he said.

That was not easy, for there were many waiters ready to dart between them, just as many heads turned to look at the lovely girl who was following M'sieur Pierre through the restaurant, wondering who she was, and why he seemed to be paying her such flattering attention. Jean, the *maître d'hôtel*, joined the procession.

Raoul came to a halt at a little round table, standing discreetly behind a bowl of flowers and ferns, and in front of a glass-panelled screen. He pulled out a gilt chair with the practice of a head waiter.

After a moment's hesitation Caroline sat down. She did not mistake the gesture, for she realized she was to be seated, but she was touched by the gentle flattery of M'sieur Pierre's action.

Then when Caroline was seated she heard the mellifluous voice saying in her ear: "Do not look so frightened, as though you are going to the guillotine. No one here is going to chop off your head and eat you. Sweet as you may be, I doubt if any of these greedy ones would prefer you to the epicurean dishes that my genius of a chef can produce." Raoul paused to introduce Jean, then he went on: "Now this morning all you have to do is to sit quietly here, to keep your eyes and ears wide open, and report to me if anything goes wrong. If you should be appealed to by Henri, who is usually in the restaurant while it is open, you must act quickly and tactfully as you think best. I shall see you later. *Au 'voir.*"

Without a backward glance Raoul went away, and after a few words Jean followed him. It occurred to Caroline that by being late she must have stolen much of his time from being usefully employed elsewhere. How foolish she must have seemed to him. What a fool she had been!

Caroline sat quietly at her little table. It was empty of food and drink, but there was a flat round rush basket filled with heavily-scented gardenias standing in a plate of water. It made her feel hungry to look at the trays of food being served so tenderly to clients at their tables, but that, of course, was her own fault. She could have eaten earlier.

Caroline kept telling herself that she must make a success of this job, though the job itself still seemed nebulous to her.

If only someone among these elegant diners, on the other side of the flowers, would pick a quarrel and create a diversion, she would show what metal she was made of. But no one seemed inclined to be vulgar and noisy, and soon she gave up the idea of hoping they would. Then it came to her that this job of hers was a delicate one. She must not look for blatant action, but for delicate shades, for hints — straws — pointers.

Sometimes Caroline was aware of M'sieur Pierre's broad-shouldered figure. His personality seemed to stand out from every man in the room, yet there were many distinguished-looking men dining at the tables. She saw that Raoul's movements were quick, quiet and unemotional. If he were ever ruffled it did not show on his face. It was Henri who was nervous, emotional and excitable. Caroline noticed that Henri and the *maître d'hôtel*, an important-looking figure, did not seem to like each other much, for once, when Henri spoke to the *maître d'hôtel*, the latter made no attempt to listen, but stood indifferently, as though he had heard it all many times before.

She knew, too, presently, that a man, sitting alone, was drinking a second bottle of champagne, with the steady persistence of a '*misérable*', trying to drown his sorrows in drink. There was nothing in that, perhaps, except that to Caroline it seemed wasteful for any man to drink alone; but perhaps the man was used to solo drinking, and obviously by the attention and deference the waiters paid him, he was a rich client.

Caroline thought: *I must not forget that I am in a different world, where money is not so important as it is in my world. What I think is a luxury, these people take as a necessity. It is a question of environment and habit.*

Caroline turned her attention to a fascinating couple who had just come in, and who were received with great *empressement* by the *maître d'hôtel* himself. She guessed they might be South Americans. The girl was dark, petite and wore the usual mink coat over her silk suit, and a small, exquisitely cut simple bonnet on her glossy hair.

Caroline wondered if they were engaged or married and on their honeymoon, for the man was obviously deeply in love with the girl and did not seem to care who knew it.

Though duty made Caroline look around her occasionally, her eyes were drawn as if by a magnet to the couple. It was delightful to watch their love story spread out before her like a fairy tale. *How lovely to be cared for like that*, thought Caroline and sighed inwardly.

She looked around the restaurant for the arresting personality which had already made such havoc in her own heart.

She did not see him. Raoul did not come near her.

Caroline's eyes returned to the entertaining couple. The man was superintending with care what the waiter was serving on the girl's plate, and pointing out a titbit that he wished her to have.

Then, like a part of a film in a cinema, she saw two stalwart waiters pass across her line of vision. They were remarkable because though they had come through the service doors, neither was carrying plates and dishes. One was carrying a pair of crutches.

Caroline let them pass without really seeing them, then caught by the unusual in them she glanced quickly a second time, and followed their movements. To her surprise they went straight to the table occupied by the man who was drinking his second bottle of champagne.

The waiter who had been attending him was standing by, holding a chit on a plate, as though presenting him with *l'addition*. There was nothing awkward in that.

In the passing of a few moments, Caroline saw the two waiters who had just entered come to a halt on either side of the man. One bent and offered him the crutches. Then, as the man started to rise, they took him by the arms and helped him gently through the crowded restaurant to a side door. At the same time his own waiter followed carrying the crutches.

His passing was scarcely noticed.

Caroline was full of sympathy for the man.

So that is his sorrow! she thought. *Poor man!*

She did not see what happened on the other side of the door, but she could guess that those kindly waiters gave him full attention, and she hoped he rewarded them. Neither did she see those tall waiters again.

After a while Caroline became bored and tired. The soft lights and the drone of that humming noise which was made up of the talk and laughter of many people, made everything seem unreal and dreamlike. The waiters, passing regularly to and fro, were moving like automatons. Caroline stifled a yawn. The heady scent of flowers made her feel faint. She touched a pure white petal of a gardenia to see if it were real, and presently, in a somnolent state of mind, she noticed that where her fingers had touched was brown. She was aware of an empty feeling within her, and then she felt sick because the smells of the various dishes that had come to her in the air disturbed by waiters passing in a continuous procession carrying trays laden with food, and which hitherto had teased her nostrils and appetite, were suddenly cloying and horrible, so that the very thought of food was nauseating.

After that the period before the restaurant began to empty was one of torture for Caroline. Food, flowers, the general atmosphere of the place, even the sight of people eating so contentedly, made her feel queasy. Sometimes she looked at a clock over the service door behind her, and thought the time would never go.

When at length the door was closed on the last client, and Caroline was free to go, she rose to her feet slowly, moving heavily and tiredly with all the spring gone from her.

Someone touched her arm from behind, and through a haze she heard Henri's voice speaking in French.

"There is nothing more to wait for down here this afternoon, mademoiselle," he said. "Go upstairs to the office where Nini is waiting for you, put the cash-box in the safe, and go home and rest."

Rest! She had an art class at four o'clock which must not be missed.

Caroline went upstairs, using the staircase because the cleaners were busy in the lift which must be left spick and span, ready for the evening. Up and around slowly she went, until she reached the top, and went along the passage to the office. She was surprised to find it was bright daylight up here, and though the morning sun had moved around and no longer beamed through the window, Caroline saw it shining in a sparkling fashion on the grey waters of the Seine, so that the river seemed to dance in the sunshine.

Nini was waiting for her in the office. She was dressed for the street, and anxious to go. She was holding a box of notes with an elastic band around it, and two small canvas sacks of money. She looked impatient, and almost flung the money at Caroline saying in her clipped, Parisienne, high-pitched voice: "You must be quicker, ma'mseile. I have to catch a train. I always have to catch a train. You do not appreciate that I, too, want to get home as soon as possible."

"I am sorry, Mademoiselle Dogas."

Nini was mollified. "Then do not let it happen again or I must report you to my Union," she threatened.

"Don't do that, please," Caroline begged, thinking that such action would start a strike.

She took the money gingerly, and went over to Nini's desk, prepared to count it; but as she turned the door was banged, and looking around Caroline saw that Nini had gone, and the room was empty.

There was nothing for it but to open the safe and put the money in until the evening. Without counting the cash, Caroline put it away, and quickly closed the heavy door. She had never handled so much money in all her life, and was afraid of the responsibility.

Presently she went into the *boudoir*. Here again she was the last person to go. Everyone seemed to have vanished. There was a sense of emptiness about the place.

Caroline looked at the three dress boxes, still corded as they had been when sent out of Toinette's *atelier*, mute reminders of the evening to come, when the hours were far longer than the lunch hours had been, and Caroline's spirit quailed suddenly.

It was then that the dream-like quality of life which had clouded her reasoning for the last three hours seemed to fade, and reality came back to her.

Caroline put on her hat and coat, and went out into the passage. She was tired and depressed.

I can't go on with it, she thought desperately, but even in her desperation Caroline knew that she would go on, not because she liked the work, but because working in this restaurant gave her a chance of seeing Raoul Pierre.

She thought, too, dizzily: *Where is he? Why haven't I seen him?*

As though the fates heard Caroline's wish, and decided to grant it, Raoul Pierre came up in the lift.

He saw Caroline at once, and frowned. "Not gone yet, Miss May?" There was reproof and annoyance in his tone.

"I am just going, M'sieur Pierre," she replied quickly, aware that he thought she was slow, and trying to hurry if only to please him.

Raoul came to a halt in front of Caroline, barring her way, so that unless she pushed past him it was impossible to move.

"How did you get on today?" he inquired indifferently, as an afterthought.

"Very well," Caroline replied briefly, trying not to let him see how tired she was. Purposely she stared at the thin platinum-bar tie pin he was wearing. Her lids felt weighted, but it was not only tiredness that made them so.

"Nothing untoward happened?"

"Oh, no."

"That is strange," he commented after a pause.

"Why?"

"Because in my restaurant something always is happening. One expects it. That is life."

"Well, it did not happen today," Caroline answered with dogged persistence. There was a pause. Caroline was so certain. One could not flatly contradict her without being rude.

"You look pale," Raoul said suddenly.

"Do I? I am always pale, m'sieur," said Caroline distantly, annoyed that he noticed her looks only to disparage them.

"But not like this." Now Raoul was genuinely concerned, sure that Caroline was concealing something from him and not liking to be thwarted.

"I — have a headache."

"I am not surprised. You must be hungry."

A faint, irrepressible shudder went through Caroline. "Please don't speak of food," she begged in a low voice.

"No! Why not? Do you not like food?"

"I hate it," was the vehement reply, with an urge of nausea at the back of it.

Raoul looked grave. "Hate is a strong word, and I do not believe you would use it lightly. I did not know that you had this feeling against food or I should not have dreamed of offering you work that would hold you in such close contact to it. You certainly could not have enjoyed yourself those three hours. It must have been an ordeal."

Caroline was silent, hurt by the sudden coldness in his tone, yet feeling too weary to explain so that he could think better of her.

"It has been rather a strain," she told him faintly.

Raoul looked at her keenly. She looked all in.

Suddenly his hand shot out towards her, his flexible fingers closing like steel on her arm. "Come with me," he ordered, at the same time holding her tightly, and propelling her into the office.

"Please let me go. I want to go home. Please."

The pressure on her arm did not slacken. It is doubtful if Raoul heard her.

"Sit down." He pushed her into a chair. Only then did he release his hold. "Relax," he ordered.

Raoul went over to a cupboard and took out a bottle of Schweppes and a glass. Opening the bottle he poured its contents into the glass, and carried it over to Caroline. "Drink this."

His orders had the crack of a pistol shot in them. His voice, usually so soft, was hard and entirely without emotion.

Perhaps because of this, Caroline obeyed like a child.

Then, without warning she leant forward in her chair, and putting her arms on the desk cradled her head in them. It was dark and restful. It was a relief to 'let go'.

Caroline did not cry. That relief was denied her. She did not even think. The attitude rested her tensed nerves.

"You are not crying, mademoiselle?"

The anxiety he was feeling pierced her mind.

"No." The sound was muffled but unmistakably clear.

The room was silent for a long while — a silence broken only by the rhythmic ticking of the little French clock standing on the mantelpiece.

Presently, feeling better, Caroline raised her head. "I am sorry, m'sieur," she said in some confusion. "I don't know what made me behave so foolishly. I have never done it before." She spoke to Raoul's back. He was standing, looking out of the window, his hands plunged deep in his trouser pockets, waiting for her to recover. "Please forgive me."

He turned as she spoke and came over to her, not taking his hands from his pockets. He sat down on the edge of the desk close beside her, saying: "There is nothing to forgive, child. The fault is mine. I should have known how it would be this first day. You are ill-prepared. You are hungry and therefore tired."

"You are very kind, m'sieur." It was all she could think of to say.

She had expected a scolding. In a way she would have welcomed a tirade. This softness and kindness touched her so that she was perilously close to tears.

"Perhaps this work will be too much for you. I do not know." Then he rang a bell which was answered by an old servant, and ordered him to get a plate of chicken sandwiches and some white wine. "Get it from the buttery and bring the tray here to mademoiselle. *Vite, vite!*"

When the man went away to do his bidding, Raoul said to Caroline: "You are to eat every crumb and drink all the wine. Rest here as long as you like." He glanced at his wristwatch. "I have to hurry away to a conference, and must leave you. Will you be all right?"

Without waiting for an answer, he went out of the room, but came back to say, "You must be here tonight in time to eat your dinner."

Caroline nodded meekly. She would never be such a fool again as to go without a proper meal.

"And of course dressed for the evening," Raoul told her.

"Yes, m'sieur." Then she reiterated, "Thank you, you are very kind."

"Not at all," Raoul replied brusquely.

Having eaten and drunk, Caroline felt suddenly better. It was not only the food and drink that made her feel so, but the fact that Raoul had noticed how tired she was. He had cared enough for her well-being to order this meal.

Of course, common sense warned Caroline not to read any special meaning into this kind act. All Frenchmen were naturally polite to women. It was their way.

But Caroline was starved of kindness just then, also she was newly in love, and longing to catch any sign from Raoul that he was interested in her. So far, she had found nothing in looks, action or speech to lead her to think Raoul was fond of her. Wishful thinking, however, coloured all her daydreams.

Caroline's confidence quickly returned, and with it a sense of happiness. With lighter step she went into the boudoir and made up her face afresh, repairing the ravages of her tiring three hours' wait in the restaurant. She exchanged a few words with a blue-overalled cleaner who was machining the carpet. Then, without seeing anyone, Caroline went downstairs and out into the street.

CHAPTER VII

Fanny was in their room. She was changing to go to a party.

"Hello, I didn't know you were going out so early," exclaimed Caroline on seeing her.

"It is only to my Aunt's in the Passy district. She has just returned to Paris from New York, and is meeting all her friends in one go. You are home early from your art class?"

"I didn't go."

"Why ever not?"

"I don't know. I was tired. By the time I was free it was too late."

"I don't blame you, honey, but don't forget if you miss too many classes you won't pass your exam."

"I know, that's what is worrying me." But Caroline did not look worried. "I don't often take a holiday."

"Well, have a cigarette, and tell me all about your job while I change."

Fanny was a critical audience. Partly because she could not bear criticism just then, Caroline began to speak gaily and rapidly.

"There isn't anything to tell. I sat for three solid hours at a little table in the background, staring at people eating and drinking. I suppose they were enjoying themselves or they wouldn't have been there, but I was too far away to hear what they were saying to each other. I had masses of flowers about me. Once I had a horrible feeling that I was a body, and the flowers had been sent to me by sympathetic friends. But I have learnt one thing, I earn every sou of the money they pay me. It is the most boring job in the world. I hope it will be better tonight."

Her tongue was running on and Caroline, realizing that she was talking nonsense solely to keep Fanny from asking pointed questions about Raoul, stopped speaking suddenly, and yawned.

Neither the brightness nor the pretence of boredom deceived Fanny. Her eyes sparkled wickedly as she exclaimed with horror: "How awful! I must tell Georges about this."

"Oh, please don't."

"All right, I won't. And then what?"

"Nothing. Absolutely nothing."

"That is dull. You poor thing!" Fanny's mind turned to more amusing things. "Have your dresses arrived from Toinette's?"

"Oh, yes, I saw the boxes in the office. They were removed to the boudoir."

"Boudoir!" Fanny's eyes widened.

"That is what they call the rest room reserved for the female staff."

Fanny nodded. "It would be just like Raoul to provide that." Then she said, "Does he like the dresses?" Fanny was intensely curious about the clothes.

"M'sieur Pierre hasn't seen them."

"How do you know?" Fanny asked disbelievingly.

"They haven't been opened."

Fanny was disappointed. "There's no fun in wearing a model dress if no one admires it."

"I don't expect to have fun in them. They were bought by the firm for business," Caroline said primly, but she sighed inwardly. It would be nice to have fun in one of those dresses.

Fanny laughed suddenly. "Shucks!" she cried, and there was a mocking light in her eyes. "One of these days I'll get Georges to take me to 'Maintenon', just so we can admire a dress, and see for ourselves if you are a good girl at the top of the class."

"Yes, do come. I shall look forward to seeing you." Caroline finished her cigarette. She said calmly, "I am going to have a bath."

"I can see you are going to make an evening of it."

"My first evening at 'Maintenon', my first evening at work, and certainly the first time I have ever worn a model dress. The only evening dress I have is one which was remodelled from my grandmother's wedding dress by our village dressmaker at home. Can you wonder I am wildly excited?"

"Then this is an occasion," said Fanny. "Use a couple of my bath sachets. Remember you've got to live up to the dress. Raoul will want you to show off. You'll have to strut about like a mannequin."

In amused silence Fanny watched Caroline draw her dress over her head, shake the dust of the day off it and put it on a hanger in the huge Breton *armoire* which they shared for a wardrobe.

Caroline put on a wrap, and picking up her sponge, soap and towel, arranging a plastic cap over her hair, and taking a couple of francs for gas from her purse, she went out of the room.

The room was in darkness, and Fanny had gone, when Caroline returned, pink, warm and damp, and refreshed by the bath. She felt calmer now, her mind more reasonable, and not so excited about the evening, which was almost upon her. Caroline knew she could cope with things. She was happy, too, at the thought of seeing Raoul again.

Of course, Caroline had reasoned to herself as she lay in the hot bath scented lavishly with Fanny's exotic bath sachets, it was no good going around at the 'Maintenon' looking like a wilting lily because she happened to feel hungry and tired, especially when they were the result of her own stupidity. That kind of thing must never happen again. Men like Raoul, who in the nature of things, if only because they are fine, handsome men, and know the trick of putting women on a pedestal, and letting her know subtly that she was there and they were far below looking up at her, were bound to be a little spoiled by women. It was inevitable and she must not be jealous. Besides, such men were fastidious in their likes and dislikes, and would never fall in love with women who were 'dying ducks' before the first breath of adversity. She must keep up her health, strength and spirits, and be a little gay and reckless, even it if were a pretence, because it was important to seem interesting and be attractive in his eyes.

Caroline dressed with care, well aware that she must pay tribute to the lovely dress which seemed more like a dream come true than anything she could remember. All her life she had longed to wear lovely clothes, but long ago she had given up any idea of such luck coming her way.

Yet luck had turned. Some of her dreams were coming true. She was happy and confident.

She put on her day dress and a long coat, and pulled on a small close-fitting hat, because there was no point in attracting attention when travelling by Metro.

And so to the left bank of the river, to 'Maintenon'.

Caroline was the first of the women staff to arrive for the evening's work. She was glad, for it gave her time to change before anyone came.

She was dressed and admiring herself with shining eyes in a full-length wall mirror, when another woman entered the room. She was a little old lady, and looked mousy, drab and undistinguished in her street clothes.

She was a cloakroom attendant downstairs, and Caroline had not, of course, seen her. They spoke to each other in French. There was nothing remarkable in what the old lady said except that she lived alone in an apartment close to the restaurant, and that Maurice, the doorkeeper, had to take her home every night.

"I like to get here early so that I can dress quietly before the young ones come," said the old lady.

Caroline was so occupied looking at herself she did not at first notice that the old lady had taken off her street clothes and was putting on a uniform.

It was only when she came to the mirror to see that all was right Caroline noticed what had happened. The old lady had changed into a black silk dress, with collar and cuffs of real lace, and a snowy mob-cap, its frill edged with the same delicate cobwebby lace, and a small apron to match. Something else had happened besides the change of clothes for the old lady was no longer mousy-looking, but had taken on the patrician air and looks of a French aristocrat. She was tiny as a doll, with shell-like, blue-veined hands, and a small face like a cameo, with bright bird-like eyes, and a high-bridged nose. She was small and delicate as a piece of rare china.

Caroline was suddenly aware of the rich dress, the fine muslin and the exquisite lace.

"You look beautiful, madame," she cried involuntarily, staring at the little figure, fascinated by her fragility, as much as her clothes.

"They all say that, ma'mselle. That is why I am chosen to be here. But call me Louise. Everyone does."

Caroline thought, *So the firm has paid for her get-up, too, as it pays for Maurice's uniform, and mine.*

A copy of old lace was not good enough for M'sieur Pierre. It must be the real thing. Caroline saw the effect such a grand old lady would have on the patrons who came to 'Maintenon'.

It shed, too, a new light on M'sieur Pierre's astute brain. He certainly understood human nature. That was why he had ordered model dresses for her. Anything 'off the peg' in a store, or a mere copy of a model, was not right for his purpose.

Then Louise clapped her hands and smiled, crying, "*Ravissante!*"

She touched Caroline's dress with gentle fingers, boundless admiration in her bright eyes. They stood side by side before the glass, the tiny Louise, like a pocket edition of something old and beautiful that had stepped out of a picture of bygone times, and the willowy Caroline: the one dressed in black and white with carefully dressed snowy hair, and the other in black shot with a burnished gold thread which seemed to flame as she moved. It was the colour of the girl's spectacularly bright hair, that exacting auburn shade which has to be studied so carefully when choosing a colour.

Caroline laughed with enjoyment. She hummed a song, a fragment of one of those being whistled on the boulevards. She danced and twirled about the room delighting in the 'feel' of the dress against her legs, and because she felt light-hearted, and adored the new dress which appeared to suit her so well, but also because she was in love.

Louise egged her on, telling her that M'sieur Raoul would think her ravishing and exquisite. The suggestion went to Caroline's head. It was as if a spirit of mad gaiety entered Caroline, and recklessly she let herself go.

A red light blinked on the wall. It had probably been doing that for some time, before Louise saw it, and drew Caroline's attention to it.

"*C'est*, M'sieur Pierre," she cried shrilly. "It is for you, ma'mselle."

Caroline stopped dancing, and her face sobered, but she still breathed quickly.

Within seconds, her heart beating tumultuously, as much from apprehension and excitement as from the unusual exercise of the last five minutes, Caroline went into Raoul's office.

He was standing with his back to the door, looking out of the window at the lights of Paris which were already pricking the greying dusk with yellow lights.

The office was brilliantly lit, like the lights in a theatre are switched on before the curtain goes up on a play. It was a dramatic moment.

At the sound of Caroline's entrance, Raoul turned round sharply, and the hands that had been hanging loosely at his sides were suddenly clenched.

He wore a dinner-jacket with a soft-fronted pleated white shirt.

They stood looking at each other in silence, Caroline's soft lips parted in a shy smile. She had not as yet controlled her breath, but her cheeks were flushed with the exercise in the boudoir. She made an attractive and unforgettable picture.

Raoul did not speak. A curious expression had crossed his face at the sight of Caroline. A nerve twitched in his cheek. A strange light glowed in his dark eyes as they rested on Caroline in her new dress. It was like a man who sees a vision, and lasted but a moment. Then his face was impassive. Purposely he made it so for this was a business interview. Slowly his eyes travelled from the remarkable coloured hair downwards to Caroline's feet. It was as though in those few privileged moments while Caroline was 'on parade' Raoul was memorizing the details that went to make up the personality of Caroline May.

It seemed a long while to Caroline. She felt anxious for her success in his eyes. Did he like her dress or not? She had no idea what was going on in his mind, for Raoul's face was now like a sphinx. It was impossible to read his thoughts. His eyes were dark and moody.

"I rang for you several minutes ago," Raoul said in a hard voice that grated unpleasantly on Caroline's ears. "You seem out of breath. Were you downstairs?"

"I am sorry, M'sieur Pierre," Caroline replied in her clear voice. She was disappointed with her reception. She had expected him to praise her dress. He must know, too, that she was in the boudoir, or why did the bell ring there? "I was in the boudoir."

"Oh! But you have been hurrying?"

"No, I was dancing."

"With whom?" How sharp this man could be!

"With no one."

"You surely were not dancing by yourself?" His tone was one of disbelief.

"I was. Louise was looking on."

"Oh!" His face cleared then, though his eyes were still fixed on her moodily.

"Are you not pleased with the dress?" Caroline heard herself asking.

"Pleased!" Raoul echoed in a puzzled kind of way. He hesitated, seemed about to speak, then changed his mind and said something else in a voice devoid of feeling. "Of course you look nice. Toinette is an artist — a genius — and knows exactly what I wish you to wear, something dark and not too décolleté; a dress which does not look as though the firm has provided it for you." Raoul paused then added deliberately, "A dress that a girl with your looks could perhaps buy for herself."

At first Caroline did not catch the full import of Raoul's studied words. She was still confused and excited with her exquisite dress, but also because she was near him.

In the silence that followed Raoul's remark, when the full import of his words dawned on Caroline she stepped back a pace from him flushing deeply.

Her anger rose. How dare this man stand there impudently staring at her, insulting her! Did he think because he happened to be her employer that he could say what he liked to her; and because of that position she must take it and say nothing?

Caroline was about to speak hotly, to tell him angrily that she was not that kind of girl, but she remembered in time that it was in his power to send her away, to dismiss her, and she could not bear that. She remembered, too, that probably M'sieur Pierre did not care if she was. The thought made her wretched but she refused to dwell on it. Such an insult must not be allowed to pass. She would demand his respect. It was her due.

She said stiffly, her mouth curled mutinously, "Do you believe I should care to buy it that way, m'sieur?"

Raoul paused, then he shrugged. "I do not know, Miss May. I spoke from a business point of view. What I think or you think is of no account. It is our patrons who count."

Caroline nodded. "I must remember that," she told him coldly.

Caroline tried to understand that everything between them in this restaurant must be regarded from an impersonal viewpoint. She was merely a minute part of the intricate machinery of running a restaurant successfully.

Just then Nini came dashing into the room. She stopped short at the sight of Caroline, and stared with unveiled hostility in her big black eyes. She had known what to expect when she saw Toinette's dress boxes, but she had not expected anything as beautiful as this, and she was furious.

Swiftly her glance went to Raoul who stood, cold and aloof, beside his desk, and she raised her eyebrows significantly. *What next!* she seemed to be saying.

He took no notice of her at all.

For a short while Nini continued to stare at him. She was thinking furiously. She dared not show her jealous feelings to Raoul. She might sometimes be short with him, though he had to be in the right mood to put up with any whims. But not now. He was definitely unapproachable tonight. She dared not risk a quick remark at anyone's expense. But through her thoughts there emerged a great hate for Caroline, because she was a rival, and lovely, but most of all because she was given every chance of displaying her charms in a new dress bought at Raoul's expense. For Nini, more than anyone, was aware that whatever might conveniently be put down in the firm's name, it really was Raoul who was responsible. He *was* the firm. The firm *was* Raoul Pierre. What he said — went. So she set about destroying some of Caroline's complacency.

She thought swiftly, for time was short. As usual, she had arrived at the last moment before Raoul would go downstairs.

She spoke rapidly in French and with much gesticulation calculated to give her words dramatic effect. "M'sieur Pierre?"

"Yes, Nini." Raoul gave her only half his attention.

"May I speak to you privately? It won't take long."

Raoul frowned at the request, but walked to the other side of the room, away from Caroline, and said shortly: "This is private enough. Go ahead."

Nini said with mock gentleness: "I have to confess. I did not wait to count the contents of the cash-box this afternoon with Miss May. I had a telephone message from home to say that my mother was ill, and I could not wait."

Nini side-tracked with unimportant details, and Raoul brought her sharply back to the point. She came with apparent unwillingness, memorizing the lies she was spinning, for a liar must have a good memory.

He listened gravely to all she said, mentally cutting out all extraneous words as she spoke, not wondering why Nini was building up a tissue of lies about the money. Raoul knew that she was trying to belittle Caroline to him and why. Nini was jealous. Loyalty to the firm or himself was as nothing to the wild jealousy that was consuming her. As he looked and listened Raoul recalled that Nini's father was a Corsican who thrived on vendettas. When she had finished, Raoul fixed cold eyes on her, saying calmly: "If you could not have found me, then you should have consulted M'sieur Henri. Miss May is new here. She has yet to learn how important it is for each person to check all money that passes through her hands. You should have explained this to her, Nini."

"It is not my place, m'sieur," cried Nini stormily.

"No, but in fairness to all of us you should have told her." Raoul glanced at his wristwatch. "Is that all, for I must go?" He walked away leaving Nini standing alone in the middle of the room. "Follow me, Miss May," he ordered, and opened the door.

CHAPTER VIII

Raoul did not take the lift down to the restaurant but led the way down the steep red-carpeted staircase. Halfway down, when he was reasonably sure of not being interrupted, Raoul paused on a small landing, and turned to Caroline, saying crisply: "Did you hear what Nini said to me in the office?"

Caroline sighed inwardly, and all the pleasure and joy that had filled her heart this evening because she was near Raoul, and wearing a dream of a dress that suited her to perfection, oozed slowly away.

Now I'm for it, she thought, aware from Raoul's distant manner, and the fact that he had chosen the semi-privacy of the staircase to the rapidity and comfort of the lift, that he was about to lecture her for something she had done wrong.

"I tried not to listen, M'sieur Pierre."

"But you heard?"

"A little."

"Nini told the truth?"

Caroline sighed, "Yes."

"You did not count the cash that was handed over to you to put away in the safe?"

"No, M'sieur Pierre."

Caroline's legs began to tremble, not because she had done wrong, but because her forgetfulness had disappointed him.

"Why not?"

Caroline would not tell him that Nini had not waited to count the money. She said, "I forgot."

"So you have no idea how much money we took today?"

"No, M'sieur Pierre." Caroline looked down. *I am being put on the carpet. Well, it is a very nice carpet — red and thick. I suppose it is my own fault.*

"Look at me!" Raoul ordered sharply, yet when Caroline raised her head and looked at him, he did not meet her eyes, but glanced away. "That was foolish of you. Nini has always proved trustworthy. I have never had reason to doubt her. But she could make a mistake in her addition. Yet if a mistake was found out after *you* had handled the cash-box, *you* would have to take the blame for any shortage. You would be expected to make it good out of your own salary. You might or might not be able and willing to do so. *But,* either way, a — stigma, I think you call it, would attach itself to your name. Now do you understand why you must always be careful of any money entrusted to you?" Raoul spoke slowly and dispassionately, not angrily, or coldly. There was no feeling of any kind in his voice.

Caroline hastened to say earnestly, "I promise I will be more careful in future, M'sieur Pierre."

"All right. It is for your own sake you must be careful. Now we shall say no more about it." He smiled, and at once Caroline felt better.

They continued downstairs, and went through the empty restaurant to Caroline's table. The waiters were having their dinner somewhere behind the doors marked 'Service'. But Henri and a young waiter were standing by Caroline's table.

A spray of spring flowers lay on the tablecloth. Mimosa, gardenias and stephanotis, and some feathery asparagus fern.

Caroline was just about to ask, "Are those for me?" when she paused.

Raoul spoke. He said: "Now I shall leave you to Henri's care. You will dine together this evening, if you permit it?"

"That will be nice," Caroline said graciously. She smiled at Henri who was so delighted to see her, and made no secret of the fact that he admired her tremendously. It showed in the way he held her chair so that she could be seated, and asked tenderly if she felt a draught. Raoul went away, and Henri pointed to the flowers.

"You are to wear those, Miss May," he said in French because he did not speak much English, and unlike most Frenchmen, he was shy of trying, afraid of making mistakes.

Caroline answered in his language, "Who said so?"

"M'sieur Pierre. Please do not look like that. He has a passion for detail.It means nothing, I assure you.The cost is—"

"I know — on the house." Caroline picked up the flowers, and asked for some pins which Henri produced, and fastened them to her dress. "Do I look festive?" she demanded.

"You look so perfect — like spring."

Caroline liked Henri. He was a stimulating companion. He said: "Today you were so shy and meek, but tonight you are the most beautiful woman in Paris, so gay and adorable. It is the same girl, so it must be the new dress."

On and off during the meal Henri paid her extravagant compliments.

"Oh, stop," she told him. "You will turn my head. I feel like Cinderella at the ball. If I am still here when the clock strikes twelve I am sure that my lovely clothes will fall off, when you will see me dressed in rags."

"That was a fairy story," Henri said, "but you are real — elegant, vivacious and charming."

He had the Frenchman's flair for making a woman pleased with herself, for saying the right thing to make a girl conceited with herself, for giving her of his best.

Real she was, thought Caroline, who was a little lightheaded with all this flattery, but the meal which Henri chose from a good list of dishes seemed to Caroline like a dream. She had a cup of Royal *consommé*, a *filet mignon* of tender, sweet meat, cooked to perfection and served under Henri's stern eye, and then a sherbet ice.

It was Henri's choice for her. For himself he would have chosen something more solid, but a lady might not care for too many main dishes at one meal.

"How will that suit?" he had asked when giving the order.

Caroline laughed. "It all sounds a little gay," she said, adding to herself, *and unreal.*

Henri was an excitable man, and a beautiful woman seemed to go to his head like strong wine, so that he felt a little uncertain of himself.

He replied, "Then we will make it a little gayer and share a bottle of claret," and he ordered in a pompous voice a bottle of Chateau Marberzet.

"Is this allowed?" Caroline asked.

"We are allowed a carafe of red or white wine free, but you would not care for that. It is not for your palate. There is nothing to stop me ordering what I like if I pay for it," Henri explained, rather truculent because he found it necessary to explain.

"There will be just time for us to toast each other," he said, adding sadly, because to him the dinner seemed meagre and inadequate, and he knew he would feel hungry before closing time. "I should have liked you to have some wild trout served with orange sauce, which is on the menu tonight. It is one of the dishes for which the house is famous, but it cannot be done. It would not be possible to enjoy four courses and coffee in half an hour." He shrugged his shoulders. "We might eat it, but there would be no time for talk. One day, when we both have a free evening, I will take you to a restaurant in the Bois, where we can eat and talk at leisure."

It sounded lovely to Caroline, but she only smiled, saying: "I must go slowly, M'sieur Henri. I am not used to eating all this rich food."

"Then I must teach you to grow accustomed to it," Henri decidedly masterfully.

They had barely finished their coffee when a bell rang insistently, and Henri rose at once with a heavy sigh.

"It has been divine, this half-hour. But it is all too short. We have just met and broken the ice to friendship, and now we must part. I shall return to you often during the evening to cheer you up. *Au 'voir*, Miss May."

He would have lingered longer, with one eye on Caroline, and one wary eye on the lift door, but it opened just then, and M'sieur Pierre strode purposefully into the restaurant. Waiters poured out of the 'service' room. They were sleek, smart and quietly efficient. Everybody was suddenly alert. Henri brought up the rear of the waiters.

Raoul, followed by Jean, walked slowly about the restaurant, between the tables. Caroline told herself that he was 'looking for trouble'. She was wrong. Raoul was seeking perfection. He spoke to Jean — made a suggestion — criticized the position of a glass — inspected a thickened thread in a table napkin, and had the napkin replaced.

He did not glance in Caroline's direction, but when he had finished his inspection, strode towards the foyer where the first patrons of the evening were assembling.

Caroline watched the restaurant fill. The lights and warmth, the smell of food and the scent of flowers — the general atmosphere of the restaurant — gave her a feeling of unreality.

The wine, instead of waking her with its hidden energy, unfortunately made her feel sleepy. She yawned several times.

She might have fallen into a doze which would have been a calamity, but just when Caroline was thinking of dozing for the nth time, she became aware that M'sieur Pierre, who had passed her by unnoticed several times, was making directly for her table.

At once, like the waiters when m'sieur appeared, Caroline became alert. Her table had been cleared long ago, but on the stretcher below the serving table, against a pillar close to where she sat, there was the empty claret bottle and the coffee-tray, waiting no doubt for a *commis* to take it away when he had time. Perhaps their waiter had not yet checked up on his commission for corkage, and until he had the *commis* would not move it.

As he came up to Caroline's table, M'sieur Pierre's keen eyes rested for a second on the bottle. He said nothing, only his mobile lips tightened with the angry thoughts and doubts that suddenly beset him.

He stopped, and Caroline looked at him expectantly, not daring to smile in case she might do the wrong thing and appear to be familiar to him in public.

Raoul bowed slightly. "Will you please come with me, Miss May?" he invited suavely, and there was nothing in his voice that betrayed the anger he felt over Henri ordering a bottle of wine. Of course, Henri was at liberty to order champagne if he wished; but Raoul resented any one of his staff buying wine for Caroline. It would spoil her. She might expect it every night. The idea was absurd. He would speak to Henri and tell him he was being presumptuous... The thoughts died away, for Caroline had risen at once and come round the table to his side.

Raoul gave her his attention. He had to. Her personality demanded it. He said quietly: "I wish to introduce you to some important people who have just come to live in Paris. They are Senor and Senora Dolores. He is the Ambassador here from one of the South American states."

Caroline felt nervous, wondering what role she was supposed to play.

"What do I say to them?" she asked in desperation as she moved slowly away from the haven of the glass screens and the shield of flowers.

She was aware that people were looking at her, commenting upon her appearance, and wondering who she was, and why she was there.

Raoul did not stop or hesitate, yet sensitively Caroline was aware that he was surprised and annoyed at her question.

His face was expressionless as he said: "I do not understand, Miss May. You do and say as you would to any of your father's friends, when you meet them in the *salon* of the Rectory at home, what any woman might say to a guest in her house."

Caroline flushed at the reproof, but it steadied her at once.

Many admiring glances followed the couple as they walked towards a prominent table at which were seated two handsome people who watched their approach with interest.

In her nervousness and excitement, Caroline would have hurried, but she could not outpace Raoul, whose step seemed to her, in a fever of impatience to get this fresh ordeal over, deliberately funereal.

She thought with annoyance, *Why is he so slow?* She thought too: *I am a failure. I have no poise. If I live to be a hundred I never shall have any. It is no good, I shall only make a mess of everything. He wants me to act. If he would only let me be myself.* Then she thought again grimly, *But if I were to be myself I should probably horrify him.*

101

She swerved adroitly to avoid a waiter who was carrying a heavy tray balanced on one hand held at an angle, but Raoul kept straight on, and the waiter had to turn aside to avoid a collision.

To Caroline, that slow progress across the restaurant was interminable. It might have seemed leisured and easy to the onlookers. To Caroline it was torture. She felt all wrong. Her feet seemed to have lost a guiding power. There was no coordination in her movements. It was a marvel she did not trip.

At last they reached the table. Caroline saw that it was flower-decked. A bottle of champagne lolled at an angle in a silver pail of crushed ice.

The Ambassadress was silver-haired. She wore a mauve silk dress which suited her to perfection. The usual mink coat was flung over the back of her chair. As Raoul said Caroline's name, she stretched out a plump little hand to the girl, saying smilingly: "M'sieur Pierre sent us a special invitation to come here tonight. He said there was a surprise for us. He did not say that the surprise was a live one, or that she was an English girl."

She had spoken in French with a pretty foreign accent.

The Ambassador, also silver-haired, had risen, and when he met Caroline he went through that form of greeting which all foreigners do when meeting women, and which seems so charming, flattering and respectful to English people.

Caroline was impressed. *Just as though I were a great lady*, she thought.

She answered in French, and at once they complimented her on her knowledge of the language.

Raoul asked, "How many languages do you speak, Miss May?" It was a lightly spoken leading question.

She replied as lightly as he had spoken. "Several. I have always found them easy."

The older people were simple and friendly, in contrast to their autocratic looks and bearing, and for ten minutes Caroline chatted pleasantly about Paris, her work in the restaurant ("I am here to hear complaints") and her home in Norfolk. The Doloreses had visited Norfolk. The Ambassador said he had fished one autumn in the River Waveney. It was a long time ago, but he remembered he had caught a pike, and that it was very cold. Then Raoul took Caroline away saying, "Now I want to make you known to some more patrons."

Instead he took Caroline straight back to her table.

"Was I a success, M'sieur Pierre?" Caroline asked eagerly.

"Quite. Are you looking for compliments?"

"Why not?" She spoke a little recklessly. She had been a success, and it had gone to her head.

"Because you will not get them. It is a part of your job," Raoul told her coolly.

"Oh!" Caroline's face lost its animation.

Then Raoul said, "With a little more practice you will gain poise and do well."

"That means I was gauche," she remarked quickly, for his patronizing tone irked her.

"I did not say so."

"But you meant that." Then she asked, "Why did you get them here to meet me?"

"Them? Their Excellencies. To make you known. To launch you. I have also invited the Press."

"What on earth for?" Caroline asked, startled.

"Because I wish and hope that you will be the talk of Paris by the end of a week."

Caroline was silent for a short while, then she said: "You must have been sure of me to invite the Press here on my first night. I might so easily have been a flop."

"I had faith not in you but in my judgment."

"It is the same thing."

"Perhaps. I think there is a fine distinction."

"What do you hope to gain from all this — gossip about me?"

"Business. You will fill my restaurant."

Caroline sighed. It was always business. "It is full already."

"Yes, but not sensationally full. Shall we leave it that I am having a little fun out of all this? To be full is not enough for me. I am ambitious. I would like to be a sensation with a big question mark."

So it was not going to be so easy here as Caroline had thought.

Before he left her Raoul said: "One thing you must please to remember, Miss May. When you walk about the restaurant do not move out of the way to permit a waiter to pass. It is his business to keep clear of you."

"But he might upset his tray."

"Then that will be too bad for him, for I never keep a clumsy waiter on my staff. The fault would be his and not yours. As I have picked my waiters carefully I do not anticipate that kind of thing to happen."

Would she ever do things to suit this difficult man, Caroline wondered.

"Oh, you see everything, m'sieur," she cried in exasperation.

"No, but I should like to." Then he added: "I saw you yawning this evening. That will never do. Even if you are bored you must not show it. To relieve any boredom I wish you to take half an hour's rest at nine o'clock. If you should wish it, coffee will be served to you in the *boudoir*. Nini will arrange it for you."

Caroline thanked him, but she thought, *I would rather go thirsty than ask Nini for anything.*

There was no rest for Caroline at nine o'clock.

At that time, when she would have gone thankfully up to the *boudoir*, Jean came majestically up to her table saying that M'sieur Pierre wished to see her in his office.

Jean's manner was impressive. People had been talking about this beautiful girl. He wished to take part in her personal success, and escorted her proudly to the lift, through a lane of admiring people, making Caroline feel like a queen.

She missed the heady attention upstairs. It was quiet. No noise seemed to penetrate. With a chill feeling in her heart, a kind of premonition that she was going to hear something unwelcome, Caroline went into the office and found Raoul working at his desk. It was irritating to see that Nini was seated at her desk in the corner. She seemed to have a malignant influence on Caroline, who was sure now that she was going to hear of several mistakes she had made — mistakes were endless, it seemed.

When Raoul looked up, she knew by his face that her worst fears were realized. He did not smile at her, or look serious. He was angry. The soft mouth was hard and drawn into a thin line. He came to the point at once.

"Sit down, Miss May." He waved his hand, indicating a chair.

"I would rather stand."

"Sit down, please."

When she did so, Raoul tapped the pad on his desk with angry fingers.

"When I asked you this afternoon if you had observed anything untoward in the restaurant during the lunch hours, why did you report to me that nothing had happened? You remember that I queried your reply, but you persisted in your reply, and I had to accept your word. But it does not agree with Henri's report."

Caroline stared wide-eyed at Raoul's face. "But nothing did happen, M'sieur Raoul, I assure you," she told him earnestly.

"Then Henri must be lying."

"Oh, no. I am sure he would not do that."

"It is what I must infer if you are correct."

Caroline looked puzzled. "What did he say?" she inquired at last.

"Well, first of all, Jean and Henri do not agree together. Did you notice that they pull against each other? I am not speaking from a personal angle. I do not care. But viewed from a business angle I must care."

"No." Caroline shook her head. "It did occur to me that they might be jealous of each other, but it is nothing fundamental. I should have thought that too trivial to report to you."

"Nothing is trivial. By using tact and planning things better I could relieve a taut situation. I could do much in the beginning, but when acrimony develops into hate I can do nothing but sack the one who is the least service to me."

Caroline made no reply. There was nothing she could say — or wanted to say, unless it was that he was making too much of a trifle.

But Raoul had not finished. He was in a better temper now. The mistake was not cleared up; but looking at Caroline made him forget his troubles. She was so lovely, like a picture, and Raoul wished he could forget the whole wretched business and devote the whole of his life to loving her as he longed to love her, an emotion that deepened with each passing moment.

He said, "A drunk had to be removed."

Caroline looked blank. "I didn't see a drunken person," she told him.

"It happened right under your nose. He was so helpless that he had to be taken out by two of my men. I only hope they threw him out of the back door."

Caroline thought a moment. Then recollection came to her. Her eyes widened. "You don't mean the lame man with crutches? I was quite sorry for him."

"Wasted sympathy! He may have been lame. I do not know. But the crutches are part of a show I have arranged to be put on to hide such vulgarities from my patrons. As you were taken in I suppose it proves the good acting of my men."

"Then they were not ordinary waiters?"

"They are two professional chucker-outs."

"Oh!" Caroline was deeply impressed by Raoul's ingenuity, and stared at him for some moments in silence. Then she smiled. It deepened to a laugh. "I can't help it, m'sieur. When I think how completely I was taken in I have to laugh. How clever of you, m'sieur. How could I know the truth? I called him 'Poor man'!"

Raoul's face expressed annoyance, but Caroline's laughter was so fresh and spontaneous, her merry face so infectious in its mirth, that he found himself laughing, too.

It was Nini who brought them to their senses. The telephone bell rang and she did not answer it. Raoul turned to tell her to do so and saw that her face registered strong disapproval. Quickly he pulled himself together.

"I see it now; it was droll. But seriously, Miss May, you must try to see things from the business angle. You appear to go through your work blindfolded."

When Caroline left the office, it was too late for coffee, so she returned to her place in the restaurant, and again nothing was as she expected it to be. Their Excellencies had finished their dinner and gone away. For Caroline the remainder of the evening was spent in talking to many men. She had no need to leave her table for they crowded about it and made all kinds of excuses for speaking to her. She could not remember the trivial complaints they made and did not try to.

Seeing her popularity, women were no less insistent in making use of her services. Caroline was invited out to dinner, to the theatre, for a drive *à deux* into the country, and to visit some bar. She was asked to sponsor somebody's face powder and to sell a dog. She was offered tickets for a boxing match, the opera, and a plane flight to London. Some men asked to see her home. Many offered her drinks. Caroline refused these last because Henri had warned her at dinner that such a thing might happen, and Raoul would not wish her to accept.

By the end of the evening Caroline's head was well turned, and she was wildly excited, almost hysterical.

Raoul did not see all this going on. He had been kept upstairs telephoning on a business matter. When he came downstairs again it was to find to his consternation and annoyance that a mild revolution had taken place in his restaurant. It was as though he had left the place asleep, and someone had touched it with a magic wand, bringing it to life.

Caroline was the reigning toast. Raoul realized, with mixed feelings, that not only was he sensational in his success, but he had started a new rage in Paris. It would mean more business, of course, but he saw, too, that in its train would be many unexpected things that he would neither want nor like.

Quietly, deftly, and with the tact for which he was famous, Raoul rescued Caroline from her host of admirers.

"You are wanted in the office," he told Caroline in a low tone.

"By whom?"

"Nini."

"Oh, Nini can wait," Caroline told him gaily. She was enjoying herself, and had no intention of hurrying on Nini's account.

"Possibly, but the last train home will not wait for Nini."

"Oh!" That gave Caroline food for thought. "It won't wait for me either."

"I'm afraid not."

Caroline rose abruptly. She had been laughing at some sally from a young man, and her eyes, usually so frank and calm, were blazing like twin fires. Her cheeks were enhanced by pink spots of excitement, and her soft mouth was parted showing her perfect teeth.

The sight of her, so gloriously lovely, made Raoul catch his breath. He had never seen her like this, gay and charming and friendly with everyone.

In response to many offers to see her safely home, Caroline shook her head. "I am not going home for ages. I have more work to do before leaving here," she told them.

She walked away from them, and no one could complain of her poise or dignity. Some went with her to the lift, but she was the cynosure of all eyes.

"Come back tomorrow," they called after her.

Raoul watched her go. He did not accompany her in the lift.

By the time Caroline reached the office, reaction was setting in, and already the fun and glory that had seemed such a part of her downstairs had fallen away so that she felt dispirited and tired, yawning openly and longing for bed.

"I am not used to late hours," she told Nini amiably.

As usual Nini was in a hurry. She was dressed to go home. She held out the heavy cash-box towards Caroline. "Take these," she said.

But Caroline drew back and refused. "No," she said unexpectedly, "not until I have locked the door. You ran away before we could count the money after lunch."

Caroline calmly locked the door and put the key into her bag. She turned to Nini whose face was dark with suppressed fury. "Bring that box here. Put it on the desk. We will count it together."

It took half an hour to count the cash and put it away, work punctuated with Nini's little screams of exasperation and defiance at Caroline's slowness and ineptitude over money matters. "Imbecile!" "Rat!" "*Cochon!*" were a few of the choice epithets flung at Caroline's auburn head. The latter took little notice of the names because she was too engrossed in what she was doing. When she made a mistake, and they were frequent, Caroline's soft tones broke across Nini's angry outbursts. "I am so sorry, I seem to be particularly stupid tonight."

"You are," was the uncompromising retort; but it was not only Caroline's poor arithmetic that upset Nini, or the fact that she was kept late, it was Caroline's beauty, her manner, the attraction she had for men, and one man in particular, the new dress — everything about the girl, which made Nini so spiteful. Locking the door had been the last straw.

When the safe was shut Caroline handed the key of the office door to Nini, an apologetic smile on her face.

"Sorry I had to do that, but I could not let you run away from me again," she said.

Nini seized the key with rough fingers. "M'sieur Pierre shall hear of this," she stormed, and swore a vendetta against Caroline.

"Oh, I shouldn't do that if I were you."

"Why not?"

"It is a waste of time. I am not afraid because I haven't the slightest idea what a vendetta is."

It was quiet when Nini had gone shutting the door after her with a resounding bang. Some of the excitement and enjoyment of the evening had gone for Caroline. Nini had depressed her. It was unfortunate that she had made an enemy of the tempestuous Nini. Caroline changed hurriedly. She would have liked to take home the spray of flowers she had worn all the evening, partly because she admired their fresh colouring, but also as a memento of the first night at this new job. Then she remembered that the flowers were not hers. They belonged to the firm. She put them in water, not knowing what else to do with them. They could not be worn a second evening.

The lift had stopped working. Most of the staff had gone. Somewhere she could hear a cleaner, sounds of scrubbing, and a deep-throated voice singing out of tune. Caroline would have liked to see Raoul. She heard men's voices in the restaurant as she passed the entrance to it, and lingered, hoping he would hear her and come out. But nothing happened, and Caroline, rather sad because she had not seen Raoul to say 'goodnight' to him, went out of the staff entrance, where the janitor was nodding in his little box, waiting no doubt to lock up and go home to bed. She went so quietly that he did not see her go.

CHAPTER IX

It was dark in the narrow, cobblestoned street. Two cars waited by the staff door. There was a chauffeur in one of them. Caroline saw the glowing tip of the cigarette he was smoking. From the shadows there emerged a man.

Caroline saw him, and would have passed him by with quickened step, only he caught her arm saying in a glad, laughing tone: "At last! You are so late I thought I had missed you, and that would have been too bad. I've been waiting for ages."

It was Kit Dale. He smiled at her in the darkness, and she caught the gleam of his teeth. Caroline had forgotten his existence in the crowded and exciting events of the evening, but she recognized his voice.

"Surely you haven't been waiting for me?" she asked, conscious of disappointment, for this was not the man she wanted to talk to — or even to see.

"Of course. You didn't think I would wait for Nini?"

They both laughed.

"She's gone long ago."

"I know. What a storm fiend she is. I saw her throw a newspaper at the janitor's head on her way out."

"Oh, that was a present of the day's paper."

"Well, come on, I'm going to see you home. You aren't the kind of girl to be let loose in Paris at midnight. I was half-afraid your boss might think so, too; or that you had some special boyfriend who had arranged to meet you."

"I was going home alone," Caroline told him.

Kit laughed. "And now you are not." He cupped her elbow in the palm of his hand, and led her towards the main street. "How did you get on tonight?" he asked.

Some of the glow of her successful evening came back to Caroline and she told him laughingly: "It was like a fairy tale."

They had reached the street which was empty and gently Caroline disengaged her arm. "There is no need for you to lose your beauty sleep on my account. I shall take the Metro home."

"Do you know the time? I thought not. The last train has gone. We'll take a taxi. Do you live far from here?"

"Across Paris. You won't find a taxi here. Let's cross the bridge and pick up one on the other bank."

"Righto!" Then as they walked towards the bridge he said: "Now amuse me. Tell me your fairy story."

"It was lovely," Caroline told him enthusiastically. "There was everything one could wish for in the evening — beautiful women in lovely clothes, with luxurious furs and gorgeous jewels, handsome men, a wonderful dinner, and lots of admiration for me — flowers…" Caroline could not stop the trail of expressive adjectives that flowed from her lips as she recalled the splendour of the evening.

They had come to a standstill in the centre of the bridge, yet neither realized that they had done so. Kit was fascinated by her. They stood in a pool of light from one of the lamps, and he thought how lovely and vivacious she was.

He said gaily, when he could get a word in, "I told you it was so easy as to be no job at all."

"Yes, but you were wrong. The job isn't simple. It is much harder than I thought. It is complicated. There are so many details to master. You have no idea the mistakes I made."

"Oh, that was tough luck. Did they give you the push?" Kit spoke sympathetically, but in his heart he hoped that Caroline would be sent away, that she would not continue working under Raoul Pierre. Kit was afraid of Raoul, his looks and personality, his influence over Caroline. *He is just the sort of bloke to appeal to her*, Kit thought, watching the lights and shades of expression flit across Caroline's eager face. *I couldn't hope to compete with him because he's right on the spot to give a girl every mortal thing she can desire.*

"Good gracious, no," laughed Caroline. "That might have happened this morning before I knew what I could do. I made a great success."

"Did Pierre tell you so?"

"No, he scarcely praised me at all. Perhaps he thought it was early days to tell me, or that it wasn't good for me to get too good an opinion of myself. *He* didn't tell me. The patrons did that — lots of them."

"I shouldn't let them turn your head, Caroline. You know how the French adore to flatter a pretty girl. They mean what they say, but you must not take them too seriously."

"But I shall. I like listening when people say nice things about me. It is much nicer when people flatter to your face than to do it behind your back, so that you may or may not hear it second-hand. Now I know my value to the restaurant. It isn't for anyone there to give me the push. The question is will I stay, or go to a rival restaurant. I had an offer to do that tonight."

"You didn't accept?"

"No."

"I am glad."

"Why?" And Caroline wondered what her movements had to do with Kit.

"Because I do know something of Raoul Pierre. He has a name for solidity and fairness. You are all right with him. Of course, if you are a success you can name your own price for staying at the 'Maintenon'. That would be all right, and good business on your part. The threat of competition, too, will put the great Raoul Pierre in the place where he belongs."

There was something bitter in Kit's voice which Caroline's sensitive ear caught, and she asked soberly, "What has M'sieur Pierre ever done to you that you don't like him?"

Kit realized that he had said the wrong thing. Caroline had noticed the dislike in his tone when speaking of Raoul, and she resented it.

Kit said quickly and frankly: "That's an easy one, Caroline. I know you will understand it. Because M'sieur Pierre has first chance with you. I'm not jealous, but it is obvious that he's got everything that I haven't."

"Has he?" Her tone was quiet but there was an unmistakable lilt in her voice. Kit was giving her new hope with Raoul. "You seem so sure."

"I've got eyes, my dear."

Then Caroline shook herself mentally. There was nothing to go upon. She must try to be sensible, and make her head rule her heart in this matter, or there would be trouble and she would be unhappy.

"But not sense, Kit," she reproved, and in so doing gave him added hope. "M'sieur Pierre is a hard-headed businessman. He may be sentimental in his private life, but I do not touch that, no one in the restaurant does. I believe he could be soft and sweet to those he loved, but I am outside that. M'sieur has no interest, other than my use in attracting new business, in me. You must understand what I mean."

Kit remained troubled, but hope made him say, "I wish I could be sure of that."

"You can be." Caroline spoke earnestly. She was so certain about Raoul.

"I'd like to believe you," Kit said slowly; then words seemed to burst from him. "But you are so breathtakingly lovely, Caroline. No man, even if he had a heart of stone, would pass you over. Just to look at you would melt the hardest heart."

Caroline was silent for a while. If only it could be! If only — Then she said with a brave pretence of lightness, "Perhaps M'sieur Pierre has no heart then, just a void where a heart should be."

It was obvious that Kit was attracted to her, yet he had only seen her in drab day clothes. How much more would he admire her if he could have seen her tonight in Toinette's creation, the dress that was hanging in her locker, with the spray of spring flowers on her shoulder!

Kit stood looking down at her entranced. He was a little puzzled by her manner. It had a remoteness which had not been there when they had talked in the top passage of 'Maintenon' earlier in the day. Her thoughts were only half with him. She was soft and dreamy. Could it be that she was in love with the good-looking Frenchman? He asked abruptly, hoping by his abruptness to surprise the truth from her: "Do you like M'sieur Pierre?"

"Of course."

"He's a tyrant, isn't he?"

"Oh, no! He is strict where his business is concerned. That is understandable."

Caroline looked over the broad parapet of the bridge. The air was soft and balmy, and the river flowed like a dark silvered ribbon under the night sky, lit with a dull golden glow from the

116

lights of the City. The lamps on either bank were reflected like jagged golden streaks by the movement of the water. The fresh atmosphere was welcome after the warmth and exotic smells in the restaurant.

Caroline breathed deeply. "Isn't it beautiful?" she cried, because tonight everything about and within her seemed to have taken on a new beauty for her, and she saw life through the cosy pink-tinted spectacles of love. "What a lovely night, so cool after the stuffiness indoors, so tranquil now, so peaceful."

The contrast was all that after the hectic evening, when dressed in the gorgeous model of Toinette's, Caroline had had to keep her wits alert and sharpened to meet all the strangers who seethed about her at times. "I wish I didn't have to go back to bed and sleep. I feel wide-awake, now."

Kit suggested: "There's no hurry to go back. Lots of cafes are open. Let's find one and have a drink and talk. There is so much I want to know about you and I am dying to begin."

Caroline hesitated. She said smilingly, intuitively proving herself feminine by withholding herself from him for a time and thereby making Kit eager to pursue her, "Oh, there's no hurry."

"There certainly is," he urged. "Tomorrow you'll be booked up by all those Frenchies I saw coming out of the restaurant. You'll be a hot favourite and forget me."

"No, I won't; in any case, you'll always be associated with my first day's work at 'Maintenon'."

Kit saw how desirable she was, and the blood surged hotly in his veins. "I want other memories than that — from you," he said ardently.

It was Kit who heard a motor coming. "Perhaps this is a taxi," he said hopefully.

They both turned to face the approaching sound.

It was not a taxi, but a chauffeur-driven private car which was being driven slowly.

Kit looked away. "We shan't pick one up here now on this bank. There's bound to be one on the other side though."

Caroline made no reply. She did not hear Kit. She had felt rather than seen or heard that the car had slowed down a little as it approached them. That might have been her imagination, for the next moment it had gathered speed and was quickly out of sight. But in that pause she had seen the passenger's face.

It was Raoul Pierre.

Their eyes had met.

A queer feeling swept through Caroline. She felt weary and exhausted. Her head ached suddenly and she felt sick. When the sensation had passed Caroline recalled that there had been no sign of recognition in his face. It had been like a mask. Yet she knew he had seen her.

Recovering, she saw that Kit was moving off, and swiftly, hardly knowing what she was doing, Caroline suited her pace to his. There was a tumult in her mind, but thought was so confused with feeling that she could not think clearly.

Supposing Raoul Pierre had followed her? Had he come to look for her to take her home? That was impossible, for had it been so he would have stopped the car and told her to get in; Had she missed something wonderful at the end of this glorious and successful evening by her haste in leaving without saying 'goodnight', not giving him the chance of saying that he would see her home? The shock passed, and Caroline thought: *Oh, what's the use of thinking? It doesn't lead anywhere. I shall never know what I've missed, or even if I have missed anything at all.*

Kit spoke. He took her unresponsive hand in his own warm lingers. "Tired?" he asked.

"A little," Caroline confessed, but she was not physically weary, only mentally.

"I thought you were. You haven't spoken a word for five minutes."

Caroline rallied then. They were over the bridge now, standing side by side on the kerb. "There was nothing special to say, and I was looking for a taxi to come along."

Kit stared around him too. "If one doesn't come soon, we'll be too late for the boulevard cafes," he remarked.

Caroline could not bear the idea of having to talk to Kit while her mind was so full of Raoul. She said, more urgently than she realized, and did not know how uncomplimentary it sounded: "Oh, don't let's go anywhere tonight. Some other night, please. I'm tired. I would rather go straight home. I'm longing for bed."

Kit frowned. He looked down at her in a puzzled manner. "You've changed your mind. You were keen enough just now. I don't understand you."

"That was because I hadn't thought it out. It sounded lovely when you suggested a cafe, but I had quite forgotten that I can't stay in bed tomorrow because I have an art class at nine o'clock. Besides, I must be up early for there is a lot to do in the apartment — before I go out — cleaning and washing some clothes. I have to iron things and press my suit."

"Can't your room-mate do the chores?"

"Fanny? Oh, she isn't domestic, and would not know where to begin. She would make such a mess of the job it is quicker in the long run to do it myself."

"You seem to have made up your mind not to join me."

"I have tonight," she told him gently, for Caroline hated hurting Kit's feelings. "Ask me another evening and I shall be delighted."

119

"When?"

"I don't know. I am afraid to arrange anything in case I can't stick to an arrangement."

"You'll be booked up after tomorrow. You'll see."

Caroline had barely got inside the door of their apartment when Fanny rushed at her.

"I've waited up especially to see you," she said, and Caroline knew that Fanny, having made her a protégée by finding the job, was taking a great and personal interest in her progress. She knew, too, that by waiting up for her Fanny expected to hear a résumé of the evening's happenings. There was no way out. It would be useless for Caroline to pretend fatigue and say she must go to bed. Fanny could be inexorable when she liked.

Caroline suggested making coffee.

While it was boiling Caroline undressed. Her mind and heart were full of one person, and nothing else seemed to count. She moved about as in a dream, answering when spoken to, but for the most part her thoughts were elsewhere.

"Listen, kid, answer me straight." The voice was familiar and Caroline pulled herself up with a jerk.

"Yes?" she queried, turning startled grey eyes on Fanny who, in dressing-gown, was sitting tailorwise on the bed. She had been keeping up a running commentary about the 'Maintenon', asking and answering her own questions until she was tired, Fanny went on. "Now it's your turn. All you've done is to grunt at me like a pig, so far."

Caroline smiled suddenly, when her whole face seemed to change. "That is what she called me this evening, not once but many times."

"Who did?" Fanny lit a cigarette. She was going to enjoy herself.

120

"Nini."

"I'd like to hear anyone call *me* a pig," was the fierce retort. "It looks as though you've made an enemy there. What did you say to that?"

Caroline smiled at the recollection of her action. "I locked her in the office — but that was before she called me a pig."

Fanny was full of admiration for Caroline. "You quiet mouselike girls are deep," she cried. "I would never have thought you had it in you to stick up for yourself like that."

Having already been given by Caroline a graphic description of Raoul Pierre's secretary, Fanny had immediately taken an active dislike to Nini. Then Fanny added, "But I suppose if you took Georges from me I should call you something more than a pig."

Caroline flushed warmly at this sally and said, "You do talk nonsense, Fanny."

"Do I? Well, there's no need for you to tell me what's happened tonight. I know."

"What?"

"That you, honey, are in love."

Fanny saw at once the flush deepen in Caroline's cheeks, and noted the shy way in which the latter bent her head to hide her face.

Caroline disclaimed this fiercely. It was disturbing to find her carefully guarded secret was such a patent fact to Fanny.

"Says you!" Fanny was delighted that without any great effort on her part she had hit upon the truth. That Caroline was deeply in love was an obvious truth. She added, "And if you are *not* in love, why are you mooning about in that dreamy state with a fatuous grin on your face?"

"Thanks."

121

"Well, it *is* silly, and can mean but one thing. If you are not in love, then you were successful beyond your dreams last night and your head is turned."

Caroline seized on the suggestion; anything to take Fanny's mind off this idea that she was in love. "I was rather a success," she admitted diffidently.

"Did Raoul say so? But of course he did."

"No. It was the clients. They made such a fuss of me."

"When friend Raoul was annoyed?"

"I do not think so. He seemed to enjoy my success."

"He should. It was good business. But it probably made him jealous."

"He was not jealous."

"Of course he could not say so. Did he see you home?" persisted Fanny.

"No."

"You don't have to speak so sharply to me. It was a natural question to ask."

"I do not think so. You wouldn't if you knew M'sieur Pierre as well as I do."

"Is that well?" inquired Fanny innocently. Then she stopped teasing to say, "Success in your new line of business means the end of your artistic and university career."

Caroline would not have this. "Remember, I only took this job so that I could stay on in Paris to continue my studies. That still goes."

"For a week, maybe, then you'll stay on because of the job. Raoul will see to that. Don't forget it was I who got you this job, so I must see that no one plays you up. Success means popularity. You'll soon have so many dates you won't have time to keep them, the job, and do your lessons. You might learn to burn the candle at both ends, as I have, but you'll want some experience for that."

"I must study," reiterated Caroline.

Fanny yawned. "Time will show," she said.

Caroline spent the night in excited wakefulness, not moving much in bed for fear of waking Fanny, who was a light sleeper. There were a hundred reasons, and all of them were to do with herself and Raoul Pierre, why Caroline wanted to be alone quietly in the darkness. There was so much to face up to and to sort out which Fanny's chatter might destroy.

Caroline got up early in the morning, tidied the room and pressed her skirt while the coffee was boiling for their *petit déjeuner*. She was no longer tired through the strain of yesterday and lack of a night's sleep, for she was in an exalted state of mind, and sleeping and eating had no meaning for her.

Later Caroline took her place in class at the art school. That morning the painting master did not find fault with Caroline's work as he usually did. If Caroline had not been so much up in the air it might have occurred to her to question him.

He stood behind her watching her progress, but he said nothing at all. This made Caroline nervous, and once she asked, "Is it all right, m'sieur?"

He replied, "Passable!"

It was damning praise, and ordinarily Caroline would have felt a failure, but in her curious state of mind today nothing seemed to matter much but Raoul.

When the class was over she did not stop to gossip with the students about her work, but rushed out, her one idea being to get to 'Maintenon' in time for lunch. It was not hunger that urged her to be there on time, but a wish to please Raoul who liked punctuality. Suddenly food and drink had ceased to interest Caroline. Fanny would have known the sign and teased her about it.

As it happened Caroline did not see Raoul.

She sat down by herself to lunch at the table where she had dined with Henri the previous night. It had been an enjoyable dinner. Caroline was so starved of praise that she had lapped up avidly all the nice things that Henri had said about her, not because she believed a word of them, but because it gave her pleasure to hear them.

There were fresh flowers on the table today, a bowl of yellow and white freesias, which were heaped in prodigal profusion, as though expense were no object in the lavish display. Caroline was quickly aware by the way the staff welcomed her that they looked upon her this morning with new eyes. No longer was she a nonentity but a person of importance, someone who was an asset to the restaurant, and in whose success they could bask. Everyone wanted to look after her comfort, and to wait on her. The janitor at the staff entrance door personally conducted her to the front entrance. As if she did not know the way! Maurice saluted her smartly, and turned the swing door slowly for her to enter 'Maintenon'. Jean, the *maître d'hôtel*, whose mayoral corpulence attracted notice everywhere, invited her to choose her lunch from the long list of marvellous dishes printed in gold on the menu-card. Caroline was not expected to eat the staff lunch. She must eat of the best. Secretly Caroline would have preferred the plainer menu which the staff was enjoying. But as that was cooked by the second chef, such a choice on her part would have upset the first chef who proudly announced that he had cooked for kings and princes.

Caroline said timidly that she was not hungry.

Henri gave up part of his lunch-time to talk to her, to see how she fared, why she was not eating, and to tempt her with suggestions of his choice from the menu. He stood at her table looking smilingly down at her, and complimenting her on a first appearance of great success.

"The telephone has been ringing all the morning, mademoiselle. Jean is distracted by people wanting to reserve tables. It is not possible to say 'yes' to all of them, because m'sieur will not allow the usual patrons to be inconvenienced, neither will he permit them to be hurried over a meal in order to make room for others. If this kind of thing continues we shall have to build an addition to the premises."

Henri said all this with much gesticulation, and in the end he raised his eyebrows and spread out his hands and looked so comical that Caroline laughed.

"But why is this sudden rush of business?" Caroline asked.

Henri stared. "Is it not possible that mademoiselle does not know? To see you, of course. Why else? What would you?"

Caroline looked serious. She had no desire to be that kind of success, even to please M'sieur Pierre, for hers was a retiring nature. She did not seek limelight, or care much for it. "I don't know," she told Henri in a troubled voice.

"It is enough that we know. We can prepare for a full house tonight and all the other nights to come until the end of July. We shall manage, even if we must squeeze the tables together more, and many people will be disappointed. To be the rage of Paris means good advertisement for our business."

Caroline shook her head. "I am sure M'sieur Pierre won't like that," she told Henri.

"Ah! Now you have said something, mademoiselle. That is the curious thing. M'sieur is not so pleased as he should be, or as we are. This sudden rush of business, this popularity is annoying him. This morning, he is in a temper. So is Nini. That is understandable because she has to leave her ordinary work to answer the many telephone calls."

Caroline smiled. "I am glad you told me. I shall try to keep out of the office."

After lunch, when Caroline went up to the *boudoir* for a few minutes to titivate, she met Kit in the passage.

He saw her at once, and came forward stealthily and smilingly.

"I've been longing to catch a glimpse of you," he whispered, taking her hand and holding it for a moment between both of his, enjoying the contact. "I couldn't sleep last night for thinking of you. I don't suppose you gave me even a thought?" He asked the question wistfully.

Caroline withdrew her hand. Instead of replying to Kit she said, "Why are you so secretive?"

He looked hurt that she had ignored his tenderness, and replied with some asperity: "Because M'sieur Pierre is sticking around. I don't want to see him. He's in a devil of a temper."

"Not with me?" Caroline mentally reviewed all that she had done since entering 'Maintenon' this morning.

"With everyone it seems, so I don't suppose you'll escape. Everything's wrong, and nothing is right. M'sieur Pierre and Nini, who is also in a black mood, have been at it all the morning. What with the telephone ringing constantly, and those two sparring with words at each other across the room, I could not get on with my work. The discipline of the place has gone to pieces. I shall leave early. What about having tea with me this afternoon?"

"I can't. I go to a lecture at the Sorbonne."

"Cut it," said Kit. He did not think the lecture important.

"I did yesterday. I can't do it twice running."

A frown marred Kit's face. "I say, you're not too high-hat to go out with me after your success of last night?"

"Don't be silly."

The frown cleared a little and Kit said: "Well, that's okay. I'll be waiting to see you home tonight."

"Please don't." Caroline looked distressed. She liked Kit well enough, but had no wish to be great friends with him.

"Yes, I will. We can finish up the evening in a cafe."

"No."

"Yes."

There was no time to continue the argument, for a door opened down the passage, and Kit whispered swiftly: "It's M'sieur Pierre. I'm off." As he spoke Kit turned and ran down the stairs, calling softly, "See you tonight outside."

Without apparent reason, unless it was that shyness came over Caroline at the thought of meeting Raoul, she turned tail and rushed downstairs after Kit, but failed to catch him up.

Caroline's panic was soon over. Before she reached the bottom of the staircase she thought: *I shall not see M'sieur now. He has probably gone down in the lift.*

Caroline, calmer now, ran upstairs again, aware that she had acted foolishly, against the dictates of her heart. All night, in the art class this morning, and while she had sat at lunch, Raoul had been in Caroline's mind's eye. She had been longing to meet him again, yet the thought of seeing him just now had caused her to flee from him.

Could anything be sillier?

Caroline reached the *boudoir* without seeing Raoul. Her guess that he had gone down in the lift was right. A sense of disappointment filled her, making her feel depressed because through her own fault she had missed seeing him and hearing his voice. She had wilfully missed a chance.

CHAPTER X

In the *boudoir* Caroline made up her face freshly, then went downstairs again to the restaurant, entering the subdued brilliance of the great room with more confidence than she had done yesterday. She was five minutes late.

The place was already filled. There was the usual hum of many voices talking at once, a sound which stopped temporarily as Caroline walked slowly and smilingly to her table, then seemed to buzz with increasing fervour behind her.

She bowed to a couple she had spoken to last night, but did not stop, meaning to return later, when they had eaten most of their meal.

Caroline's table was cleared except for the flowers, which drenched the atmosphere about them with their scent.

Hardly was she seated than Raoul came up to her. He was carrying a sheaf of newspapers in his hand and put them on the table. He glanced at his wristwatch with raised eyebrows and bowed ceremoniously before he said, "Good morning, Miss May."

"Good morning, M'sieur Pierre. I am five minutes late, but I am not going to say I am sorry, or you will think I am a dumb redhead who has no vocabulary outside the word 'sorry'."

A ghost of a smile flitted across Raoul's face, and was gone. "I did not say you were late," he told her mildly, but the glance he gave her was keen, noting every detail of her looks and expression.

"No, but you acted it."

"I happen to know that you arrived on time, Miss May." Then he said, "Have you seen the papers this morning?" He flicked the bundle distastefully.

Caroline was dismayed, wondering what she had said or done to make him annoyed with her. "No, we don't take any papers, M'sieur Pierre. Anyway, if we did, there was no time to read them today. I was at the studio at nine-thirty. Should I have seen them?"

Raoul shrugged. She looked fresh and alert, as though she had slept well, and not as if she had spent hours after midnight with Kit Dale, dancing or at some cafe — anyway together. The thought of them being together made him furious.

He said: "You might like to. There is so much about you in these. I have marked the 'gossip' columns. Read them at your leisure."

"Thank you." Caroline took the papers with a feeling of elation that she could not hide. It would be lovely to see her name in print, especially if they had said nice things about her. Though longing to read them Caroline resolutely looked away from the papers. M'sieur Pierre had suggested she should read them in her spare time. That was a hint she could not ignore while he was in this difficult mood.

She asked, in a business-like tone, "Is there anything special you would like me to do or say today, anyone you wish me to talk to?"

"Not this morning, thank you, Miss May."

There was a short silence then Raoul spoke, the words seeming to burst from him without any volition on his part. "Why did you rush off without saying '*au revoir*' to me last night?"

So that was to be a grievance! By then, Caroline was deeply in love with Raoul, and it hurt to know that he was angry with her. Caroline replied, "Did you expect me to before I went?"

"It would have been polite: do you not think so?"

Caroline looked down then she raised her eyes to his. She looked troubled and pale. Things did not seem to be panning out well between them, not in the way that Caroline would have liked. "You are right, m'sieur," she admitted. "It was rude of me to run off without a word."

"I remained behind to see you go."

"Oh, I am sorry." Caroline was genuinely upset. "I heard voices when I came downstairs, I recognized yours, but you seemed so occupied, or I think I should have said 'goodnight'."

"You went out the back way. That was why I missed you."

There was a note of reproof in the soft voice, as though Caroline had done a wrong thing.

She said quickly, "I thought that was the door I must use." She would not give Maurice away.

"That was not my intention. I told you clearly you were not on my staff and why. In future you will use the front door for coming and going."

Caroline nodded to show that she had heard.

"After midnight is too late for a young girl to be alone in the streets of Paris."

"I was not alone, m'sieur."

"I know. But tonight and every night while you are working here you will go home in a car."

"Oh, I couldn't dream of inconveniencing you."

Raoul's eyes widened at her words. "*I* am not thinking of taking you. Emile, my chauffeur, a trustworthy man, will drive you in the staff car."

"Oh!" Caroline felt foolish. Had she really thought Raoul would drive her home?

"You would have seen it last night, no doubt, only you were otherwise occupied with your friend, M'sieur Dale. I am sorry that I cannot offer him a lift, too, but the car is kept for certain purposes, for the use of the staff only — or do I make myself clearer if I say it is for the use of anyone who works in this restaurant, for sudden illness, or a journey to hospital, or in bad weather, or if anyone is kept late and loses the last public vehicle which could take them?"

"I understand perfectly," said Caroline clearly.

"Perhaps when you see Mr. Dale, you will explain the position to him?"

That would be difficult, for Kit, although he was regarded only as an acquaintance by Caroline, had, because he was her countryman, they were in a strange country, and he was attracted to her, assumed an air of proprietorship which it might be hard to override, for he was a confident young man, adored by his mother, who made a fool of him.

Caroline did not reply at once. She was savouring what Raoul had just said, turning the matter over in her mind, wondering if he were jealous of Kit and trying to curtail her liberty to go out with him when work was over, or whether he really had her best interests at heart, if he cared sufficiently for her to wish for her safety.

Raoul continued in his soft voice, that Caroline loved to hear: "I hope you will not think me a sport-spoil, but you will appreciate that I cannot offer free rides to the friends of all the people who work for me. There would be no end to joy-riding if I did."

For a wild joyous moment Caroline wondered if his reiteration that Kit should not ride in the car meant that he was afraid of him as a rival, but the thought passed quickly.

Caroline said: "I will explain to Mr. Dale. I am sure he will understand. There is no reason why he should expect you to treat him to free rides in your car."

She spoke with dignity, unsmilingly, because she knew that Kit would *not* understand. He would have plenty to say about the curtailment of her freedom. He would probably throw out hints about tyrants, little dictators, and slave-owners. He would resent M'sieur Pierre's interference with her liberty hours.

"You are of age. You can do as you like. If you won't stick up for yourself and tell the fellow where he gets off, then someone must do it for you," Kit would probably say in warlike mood.

Raoul bowed. He hoped, grimly, that Kit Dale would understand the position, but doubted it. The man was an active rival and must be watched. So he said: "Dale will be annoyed. There is no doubt about that. But I am sure he will be sensible and take everything in the right spirit, as nicely as you have, sure that my desire to protect you from any harm proves that I have your best interests at heart."

"But I don't mind," Caroline told him. "I am tired at midnight. I shall be glad of a lift."

"I do not follow," Raoul said in some perplexity. "You like Dale. You appeared to be enjoying yourselves on the bridge last night."

"Did I? I was admiring the view. It was wonderful," said Caroline simply, but she searched her mind frantically for a clue as to what she was doing or saying at that vital moment last night, when Raoul saw her from his car window.

"There was no view. It was night."

"But all the lights of Paris were on."

Raoul smiled then. There was a wistful quality in it that touched Caroline's heart.

When he went away she watched him go with longing eyes, her mind full of softness and tenderness for him. The interlude, not a happy one, surely was over. Perhaps she would not see him again until tonight — hours hence.

Sudden unexpected tears filled her eyes, and she fixed them quickly on the frail beauty of the flowers in the bowl, trying not to let them spill over down her cheeks and spoil her make-up. *He would never forgive or forget it if I cried before the clients*, she told herself fiercely. *Be quiet, you fool. There is nothing to cry about. It is only that your idiotic mind expects him to feel, and act and speak like a great lover. Why should he, especially after such a short acquaintance?* The trouble was that Caroline, feeling deeply herself, wanted to rouse a similar feeling in Raoul, and felt frustrated because he did not show some sign of emotion for her.

Willing herself to be calm, Caroline looked after Raoul's retreating figure, and as she looked it seemed as though he remembered something for he hesitated, turned swiftly and retraced his steps.

Though Caroline watched his coming with inward agitation, at his approach, carefully and quickly she made her face a blank.

Perhaps he is sorry he spoke so coldly to me just now. Perhaps he will speak a few kind words, show a glimmer of gentleness, something that I can treasure in my dreams tonight, Caroline thought wildly.

Raoul stopped in front of her, and Caroline caught her breath and waited.

"Just one thing more to remember, Miss May," he said and at the coldness of his tone Caroline's heart sank. Raoul had not returned to distribute favours or compliments.

"Yes, m'sieur!" she breathed as he paused.

"There is no need for you to run away again at my approach."

It was too much for her nerves to bear, and Caroline snapped back vehemently, "I didn't." The suggestion that she was a coward hurt. Then she remembered, and corrected herself: "Yes, I did."

"There is no need for you to feel afraid of me. I may often be angry because I like perfection, and am impatient as a teacher, but I never bite."

"I wasn't afraid of you. Indeed, I do not know why I tried to avoid meeting you because —" Caroline swallowed hard. There was a constriction of her throat that must be swallowed at all costs if she were not to make a fool of herself. Her voice sounded thin and unconvincing in her own ears.

"Yes: go on."

"Oh, I can't explain." She raised appealing eyes to him.

"Why not?"

"You would not understand, m'sieur."

He stared at her angrily. Then unexpectedly he agreed, "Perhaps not."

With one of those swift changes of mood which Caroline had experienced and were characteristic of Raoul Pierre, changes which fascinated and exasperated her, he said in a pleasanter tone than he had used hitherto: "Your job is as new to you as it is to me. I expect both of us will make mistakes and need correction and adjustment, and that goes for me as much as for you. But I have no doubt we shall adapt ourselves in time to a proper working level. In the meantime we must learn to give and take. If we understand that we shall soon get along very well."

Caroline said faintly, "I hope so."

But she was disappointed. Quite what she expected him to say Caroline did not know. It was certainly not this business-like acceptance of a position, the cool explanation which any employer might make to any employee. It was madness on her part to expect a kindness and tenderness bordering on love.

Raoul asked kindly, "Did you eat a good lunch?"

"Yes, thank you, m'sieur." Her voice was small and tight.

He sighed, slightly irritated with her answer. "Jean tells me otherwise."

"Then if you knew why did you ask me?" Caroline said with spirit.

"Because his ideas and yours of a good lunch are probably different in quality and quantity. Perhaps you do not like our food."

"It is exquisite."

"Or perhaps you fancy some dish that is not on the menu?"

Caroline smiled faintly. "There could not be many left even for a connoisseur, for you have a long and varied menu, m'sieur."

"Well, is there anything?"

"No."

"Then why have you no appetite?" he persisted.

"I am not hungry, m'sieur."

"Nonsense, you must eat. I insist. It is absurd to work without proper food. I shall order a tray to be sent to the office at three o'clock."

"But I don't want anything." Then Caroline broke off because Raoul's expression was adamant, and it was useless her saying she was not hungry. He had made up his mind she must eat, and she would have to eat. So she said gaily the first thing that came into her head: "What I do fancy sometimes in Paris

135

is some tea and a slice of English bread and butter. I expect you think that rather a silly wish?"

Raoul replied: "No. You are very sensible to tell me. Now we are getting somewhere. If I can get this *tranche* of bread and butter in Paris, you shall have it. I have some tea in a caddy in my office. I do not know why I keep it for I never use it. I think it must be because the caddy is an antique lacquer box brought as a present to my grandmother from China by the captain of a sailing barque. It is a curiosity. In my spare time I am keen on seeking out old things that have 'lived' in a bygone age."

Caroline nearly said that she had an insatiable passion for doing that, but she hated the disappointment of never being able to buy a single piece of china or glass, or even furniture that she liked. But that would have seemed presumptuous. She said instead politely, noncommittally: "How interesting! I shall look forward to an English tea."

"Oh, don't count on it. I promise nothing except that I will try. Perhaps not today for I am busy, but tomorrow."

This time Raoul did go away and Caroline was left alone.

To say that Kit was furious when Caroline told him that she was being sent home by car, and so could not go with him, was understating his anger.

He asked haughtily, "By whose orders?" It was an unnecessary question for he had already guessed before Caroline replied: "M'sieur Pierre's."

"And are you taking them?"

"It would be silly not to."

"Of course you know why he has done this?"

"Because I am finished so late the last train has gone."

"Rot!" cried Kit rudely. "The man's jealous, just as I told you he would be when he knew of our friendship. We have both fallen for you, and he is quick to make sure I don't get first look-in with you. He wants to outride me, not so much perhaps because he wants you as to get me out of his way. It is a matter of pride with him. I would call it conceit. The pretext is your safety. I've heard that tale before. Take my advice, Caroline, and keep your eyes skinned against him. I've heard that he is dangerous. Now I know he is. If you would only listen to me you would leave this place at once. You are out of your element here. They don't want people like you but a show girl. Before long he'll be starting a cabaret. At the moment you are something new, and so a success, and he's underpaying you. Presently, he'll be pushing an agreement under your nose, with the odds weighted on his side, asking you to sign on the dotted line."

All this was poured out from Kit's overcharged emotions, in a swift breathless whisper on the stairs. Kit had waylaid Caroline there because it was quiet and there was a chance to talk and so improve their friendship. She had seized the opportunity to pass on Raoul's message, and Kit had taken it badly.

He had known that Raoul was his rival. It was an instinctive feeling and based on the fact that if he, Kit, admired Caroline, then all men must do likewise. It had never occurred to Kit that the next move in this game of rivals would be this.

Caroline listened in silence. She was elated, amused and angry; elated at the thought of Raoul falling for her; amused at Kit's swift tirade and open jealousy; and angry because he had called Raoul dangerous. So far he had seemed thoughtful for his staff, though he was exacting about the beginners such as she was.

With heightened colour, because speaking about emotions so openly embarrassed her, Caroline said coldly: "Please don't lose your temper, Kit. It is unnecessary. To suggest that M'sieur Pierre has fallen for me is stupid. He has not. To twist a kind-hearted action into some act of rivalry is foolish. I know M'sieur sends Louise, one of the old cloakroom attendants, home in Maurice's charge every night. She lives near the restaurant, and some men would not think it necessary for her to have an escort home. Certainly no one suggests he has fallen for her because he is anxious for her safety."

"That is one way of looking at it," cried Kit sourly. "But you may depend he is getting something out of her and does not want anything untoward to happen to prevent her service to him."

"That may be true," agreed Caroline gravely, "because M'sieur is a business man, but it doesn't lessen his kindness to Louise. He pays her well, and Louise is willing to work here and to go home alone. It is entirely his thought that Maurice must take her home."

"Then it will be okay if I tell him I will look after you when you go home."

"And will you?"

"Of course. I shall also tell him to mind his own business, and not to interfere between you and me," said Kit boldly, his courage outrunning his discretion. "If he takes it badly, or is rude, I shall walk out on him and refuse to do his work. He won't like that because he is used to my firm's way of handling his accounts."

"I shouldn't bother to speak to M'sieur about me, Kit. We are not in England but in France. Men aren't supposed to be rude to each other here. If they are they fall back on duels."

"Illegal!"

"But they are still fought. Besides, you will only get the sack."

Kit snorted. "I couldn't care less. I am a brilliant accountant and can always get a job. I don't worry."

"But *I* do. Men don't quarrel about girls nowadays. If they do it in public it is a sign of retarded growth." Then seeing she was making no progress with Kit about Raoul, Caroline had a brainwave. She said persuasively: "Why let M'sieur Pierre know how you feel about seeing me home, when we can meet on Mondays, which is my day off, or during my weekend once a month?"

It certainly was an idea and Kit's face brightened. M'sieur Pierre would not know about their meetings. Anyway, he could not interfere.

"Do you want this?" he asked Caroline eagerly.

"Well — those are my free times," said Caroline guardedly, "but I expect to be fairly busy then having a hair-do, a manicure and laundering my clothes; turning out the apartment, and catching up on my art lessons and languages."

Kit looked at her sombrely. She was changing already, putting on polish, adopting a sophisticated air, and generally improving herself. But polished or unpolished she fascinated him. He asked, "What about Monday?"

"Next Monday? Oh, I can't tie myself so far ahead."

"I knew you'd cry off if I tried to nail you down."

"Oh, no, but I must spend time on myself. I have to be well-groomed and —"

"What about lunch on Monday, Caroline?"

Kit persisted, and in the end, for the sake of peace, Caroline said, "All right, I will if you want me, and it will make you happy."

It seemed the only way to keep Kit quiet, and to avoid a scene which he might create with Raoul about seeing her home.

At the same time Caroline realized that Kit was not going to be content with ordinary friendship. He would want something more and quickly, which she definitely had no wish to grant him. How could she even enjoy friendship with Kit when her heart and mind were so full of Raoul Pierre? For good or ill, she was in love with Raoul. So she must go warily, for what seemed simple enough in her friendship with Kit could easily become complicated, when everyone might be unhappy.

CHAPTER XI

Then it was Fanny's turn to worry about Caroline.

With each successive visit to the 'Maintenon', Caroline appeared to move deeper into a dreamlike existence. She seemed to live apart. It was a love phenomenon that frightened Fanny, who viewed life prosaically at all times, whether in or out of love, her head usually ruling her heart. She could never 'get at' Caroline. No matter how much they discussed love, Fanny felt there was something about Caroline, a kind of reserve, that she could not reach. Fanny had felt the change in her friend that first night, after she had met Raoul. She had wondered then what her good intentions had started for Caroline, and where it would lead. At the moment, Caroline seemed absorbed and happy. Because love was in her head and in her heart she was blooming, desirable and lovely. Looking at her friend, Fanny often wondered, *How could any man withstand Caroline?*

But watching Caroline, late at night, when she seemed dropping with fatigue, or early in the morning, when she was only half-awake, Fanny thought she discerned many shadows in the happiness which appeared to break its serenity. Fanny decided that while Caroline's love was deepening and strengthening daily, so far there had been no sign of a return love on Raoul's part.

The man must have a heart of stone, Fanny decided with exasperation.

Caroline's loveliness had that wistful quality of defenceless youth which is so appealing.

Fanny thought, too, *If Raoul does not show his hand soon, that Kit will make headway with Caroline, for she might well turn to him for consolation.*

Of course Fanny knew all about Kit Dale.

One morning Caroline announced, "I am to wear a new dress tonight."

"What is it like?" Fanny asked with interest, because, next to love, buying new clothes and masses of trinkets from those fascinating little shops in the rue de Rivoli were absorbing matters to Fanny. She was intensely surprised when Caroline replied: "I do not know. I haven't opened the box yet."

"What! You are not interested and excited to see all your dresses? You must be a sub-normal."

Caroline laughed. "I would have looked at them long ago, and hung them up in my locker, which is the size of a small wardrobe, for dresses left in a box get creased, but M'sieur Pierre asked me not to open the boxes. He wants me to have a surprise."

There was a short silence, then Fanny said, "I see," but she look mystified. "Well, you know how to rouse my curiosity, I must say. I shall have to dine at the 'Maintenon' tonight, if only to see your dress."

Caroline shook her head. "I've wondered why you haven't been before," she said, "but you can't come tonight."

"Why not?"

"Because we are booked up for four nights ahead. We could book up indefinitely, but M'sieur Pierre won't hear of it. He wants to widen the circle of his clientele, and not have the same faces there every evening."

"I see." Fanny looked thoughtful. This popularity had only come to 'Maintenon' since Caroline was there.

As usual, when alone with Georges, Fanny talked to him about Caroline, and once more she mentioned what was worrying her. "Caroline isn't like me," Fanny said. "I know men and can take it, but Caroline has no experience."

"If I know Caroline she can take it, too."

"Perhaps. I don't want to test her. I want only happiness for Caroline. She's my friend, and must have the best. If Raoul plays her up I'll never forgive you."

"Me!" That shook Georges. Why should he be blamed for Raoul's behaviour? Not that he could see Raoul playing anyone up. "What have *I* to do with this affair?"

"He is your friend. You started all this."

"But I did not expect to be blamed if anything went wrong. Not that I think there *is* anything wrong. Caroline may be mistaken —"

"Caroline has said nothing. In fact, it is what she does *not* say that makes me think."

"It is early days yet. Caroline has not known Raoul a week."

"Time counts nothing with love."

Georges knew that to be true. "The sooner we go to 'Maintenon' and see for ourselves the better," said Georges. "From what you tell me, Caroline is not to be depended upon. We will go there tonight." Then as an afterthought, "Perhaps I'd better give Jean a ring and reserve a table."

"You won't be able to get one at such short notice."

"I think I will."

"Caroline says they are booked to capacity for several nights ahead."

"Oh!" Then, nothing daunted by such news, Georges said easily: "If I know Raoul, and I should do so, he has probably kept a few tables in reserve for old friends and patrons. I'll ring through to Nini and see what she can do."

"That's a shut door, honey. Nini hates Caroline. She won't help."

"Then I will arrange an appointment with Raoul. He is a busy man, but I know he will find time to see an old friend. So put on your best dress. We go to 'Maintenon' at nine o'clock tonight."

Georges was so confident that Fanny told him admiringly, "You are a wizard, Georges."

"Of course nothing is arranged yet," Georges said modestly, thinking it wise to prepare for failure, "but if there is a spare table to be had, we shall have it."

Fanny spoke about Caroline to her aunt, whose apartment, in the Passy district, on Sunday afternoon was the nearest approach to a *salon* that Paris could boast of.

As Fanny's student friend, and impecunious room-mate, Caroline had not hitherto been of sufficient importance for her name to be put on Mrs. Cornell's list of celebrities. But after her secretary had read the glowing accounts of Caroline in the 'gossip' columns of the daily papers, and how she drew large crowds to 'Maintenon' every night, Mrs. Cornell decided abruptly: "Obviously Miss May is a girl of distinction and charm. If M'sieur Pierre has reached the point of being 'desolated' not to be able to reserve tables at a moment's notice for favourite patrons, then she has that something which I like my friends to meet. She must come here. Fanny shall bring her. Then I shall be crowded out which means that I, too, shall be successful!" She laughed at herself and said: "That, Solange, is a form of snobbery, I suppose, but it is delightful and pleases my ego. Please put me through to my niece at once."

Nini telephoned that she had a cold and would not be coming that morning, and an old man, one of those retired people who continue to haunt the place where they have worked for years, bored with retirement, and who can be depended upon adequately to fill up a gap in the staff at any time, sat at Nini's desk.

Caroline had come early and welcomed him warmly. She liked his face. He had a friendly smile and a sense of humour. Also his being there gave her a respite from Nini's attentions which had been so unwelcome the last two days, and promised to make Caroline's stay at the 'Maintenon' uncomfortable.

Once Nini had upset Caroline's box of face powder. That might have been an accident. Nini apologized profusely, but the powder was lost. What happened yesterday was deliberate. Caroline had found salt in her pot of cleansing cream which she had left on a shelf in her locker. She had not used it, happily, because Louise had warned her of what had happened.

It was unfortunate that she had made an active enemy of Nini. Though Caroline tried to be friendly, Nini refused to have much to do with her. She snatched the receipts for money that Caroline handed to her, and had a fund of rude expressions which she used constantly if they were alone and conveniently forgot to pass on any messages from Raoul to Caroline, pretending she had forgotten, and did all she could to get Caroline into trouble with Raoul.

Today, without Nini, who was ever-watchful, the atmosphere of the office was not so business-like. There was a lack of tension which allowed for friendliness and informality.

Caroline acted as 'mate' to the clerk. She copied out names, making mistakes which the old clerk thought funny and laughed at.

"These dishes are only names to me," Caroline told him.

"And to me. But I was doing this kind of thing before you were born, ma'mselle." With the freedom of age, when Raoul was in the office, which was most of the time, the clerk repeated some of Caroline's mistakes. There was a short period of leisure while he waited for Caroline to bring him a fresh supply of paper from the cupboard.

Raoul laughed heartily, and hearing the sound — soft, tender and melodious — Caroline's heart lifted suddenly. Presently they were all three laughing with a freedom that Caroline had not known before in this office. Everything was so strictly formal when Nini was there.

Laughing made Raoul appear younger, and Caroline thought again, with that queer turning over of her heart which happened so many times during the day to her, how young, handsome and desirable this man was.

Raoul said to her, "I suppose you'll learn the work someday, Miss May."

Caroline replied laughingly, even pertly: "I hope so. I had no idea when I took it on that there were so many things to learn here. It will take me some time to understand my own funny job."

She took the paper over to the clerk. "This will last you today, m'sieur," she said.

Raoul had not replied, and struck by his silence Caroline paused to look at him. She was astonished to see that the smile which she liked so much, and which softened his expression, making him seem more human and endearing, had vanished.

Now what have I said? she thought in consternation.

The clerk, quick to take his cue from Raoul's face, was suddenly silent, and buried his face in his work, not venturing to look up.

"Funny!" Raoul repeated stiffly. "What is so funny about your job, Miss May? I should like to hear. I did not know you looked upon it as a joke."

Caroline recovered herself quickly. "Oh, I don't," she said, "I used the word 'funny' meaning odd or strange, and as you know, this kind of work is strange to me. I can assure you I have never thought of it as something to laugh at."

Caroline recalled hazily how tired she had been these last few nights, how wakeful she had been, not on account of the job, but because her mind was filled until dawn by his image, and how hard it was to get up in the morning. Indeed, what with the work, her lessons, and preparing herself and her clothes for work at the 'Maintenon', there was no leisure for rest. There was no fun in hours that had been arduous.

Raoul replied gravely: "Then it is my mistake. I told you before that my English, she is bad, and you would not believe me. It was a mistaken kindness on your part. I use too many long words. I do not always understand the meanings of the words you use, like funny, which has two distinct meanings for you. That is why I wish for lessons, to correct these wrong impressions."

Caroline nodded. Raoul's English was not perfect, especially when his emotions were roused — then he relapsed into a mixture of French and English, or only French.

She said, "We do not seem to have had any time over for English lessons, m'sieur."

"Then we shall make time."

"But when?"

"Perhaps you do not wish to teach me?" Raoul inquired suspiciously.

"I do, but —"

Raoul put up a protesting hand. He thought a moment, then he said: "After this week, it shall be easier for you. Monday is a slack day, but it is also your free day. If it were not your holiday I am sure that we should not be slack. I do not, of course, expect you to give any of that day to me, but — we shall see. I am determined to master your language but I can only do so with your help, so it seems as though we must find some spare time. It can be arranged if we wish it."

When Caroline went out of the office to make up her face before going down to the restaurant for *déjeuner*, the old clerk sighed so heavily that Raoul asked him what was the matter.

"I was but wishing I were forty years younger, m'sieur."

"Why?"

"Because I should fall in love again."

"Oh!"

"Never have I seen one in this office so good, kind and lovely. It is like sunshine in a dark room: listening to a lark rising from a meadow, or seeing the first flower of spring."

Raoul's mouth twisted humorously, and he said lightly: "You are almost sentimentally poetic. It must be the spring in the air."

"It is love. Do not you feel it, too, m'sieur?"

Raoul looked gravely impassive, and wondered why he bothered to listen to this garrulous old man. "I cannot say that I do." But his tone lacked conviction.

"But, m'sieur —"

"Enough. Keep your head. Go to your *déjeuner*. At your age food should seem of more importance than love."

"I know. You do not need to tell me, m'sieur. But every spring, for someone, it is the same cry of *toujours l'amour*."

Raoul thought the incident ridiculous, but it bothered him. It stayed in his mind until he went down to the foyer.

He was thinking about it when Georges rushed up to him and they exchanged boisterous greetings.

"Hello," cried Raoul, holding him by the arms, as one does a newly-found brother. "What brings you here?"

"Things."

"I haven't seen you for ages. What can I do for you? Now if you want lunch I must warn you we are terribly busy. As it is late some of the clients must have nearly finished, and there will soon be a vacant table. I will find out for you."

Raoul was not eager to find Georges a table. He was in a hurry to see Caroline, not necessarily to talk to her, but just to see her and to know that she was there. He had thought the clerk's remarks foolish, but somehow they had given a fillip to his thoughts about Caroline.

Raoul turned Georges towards the bar and gave him a friendly push. "Go into the bar, my dear fellow, and get yourself a drink on my account. I will warn Jean to let you know directly there is room for you."

Georges resisted laughingly. "I'll have a drink if you will join me, Raoul. I do not want lunch. As a matter of fact, I've already broken the edge of my appetite with a snack and a light lager. What I want —"

"You are in trouble again," cried Raoul quickly. "Love trouble?"

"On my honour, no."

"Is it still Fanny?"

"It is. What I want you to do is to reserve a table for two for dinner."

"When?" The two friends paused just inside the bar, and faced each other.

"Tonight, at nine."

"But that is quite impossible. Every table has been booked for several days now. Of course, Jean —"

"I have already asked him."

"And he confirms what I say?"

"He does. He is uncompromising. So I side-stepped him and came to you."

"I cannot make tables or room."

"No, but you must keep a few tables in reserve for your friends?"

"I do, but even those have gone. Honestly, Georges, I am very sorry. I should have liked to keep you a table. Come some other night. Make it the middle of next week. It will be cheaper, too, for tonight is a special dinner and naturally the prices are higher."

"No. Don't try to persuade me that next week is better than now. I am not a man of patience, as you know."

Raoul shrugged. Simultaneously they both made for the bar.

"Let us talk this out over a drink," said Georges. "Remember I savour the best of life by taking things at once. Waiting destroys flavour and zest."

"What will you have?" asked Raoul resignedly.

"You choose."

So Raoul ordered the drinks. He glanced surreptitiously at his wristwatch. "I can't give you long. I am busy, and I may be called away at any moment."

"I know." The friends leant against the highly polished counter and talked of many things. They had two drinks. Georges made no progress. He tried a more direct attack. "You are looking fit," he said in an aggrieved voice.

"Why should I not? I am in good health. My business prospers. I want for nothing."

"You are fitter than you were in January."

"Of course, I was ill then."

"So ill that I tried to find a tonic for you. You wanted plenty then."

"Yes?"

"The tonic is acting very well," said Georges slyly. "I do not need to ask if you find it palatable."

They both laughed.

"How is Caroline shaping?" Georges inquired boldly.

"There is no shape about her work, but Miss May has filled my restaurant uncomfortably full as you see. She is an asset. That is all which matters."

"Is it? If Caroline emptied your restaurant that would be wrong?"

"Yes, of course."

"Then you would get rid of her?"

"I suppose so," was the bland reply.

"Liar! You know you would not." But Georges spoke without rancour.

"What are you driving at?" Raoul looked vexed.

"You know very well. Are you in love with her? If you aren't you ought to be. She's wonderful."

Raoul frowned. "You should not have asked me that. I do not care to discuss love and Caroline May."

"Perhaps not. But you *do* love her?"

"Yes — from the moment I set eyes on her. Now be quiet. I do not talk about her and love."

"Is she happy with you?"

"I have not asked her."

"Then why don't you? Surely that is one of the first things you should find out?"

"Because — I have known her for six days only. What do you expect me to do, frighten her out of her wits by making violent love to her? She would probably box my ears and leave me."

"You will have to risk that, for if you wait too long before showing your hand, some other fellow, one of her own countrymen perhaps, will beat you to the post."

Raoul cried angrily, "What do you know about that?" He looked quite pale, and clenched his hands.

"Nothing, but Fanny and I are worried about Caroline. That's why we want to dine here, to see for ourselves what is happening, and to get at the truth. We are your friends, Raoul, and want to help you."

Raoul said grimly: "You shall have a table. It will be waiting for you at nine o'clock tonight." And he thought, *Georges will let me know if there is anything between Caroline and Dale.*

"What a pal you are, Raoul."

"I hope you are, too," was the significant reply.

"I am," was the fervent rejoinder. Georges had had three drinks. He was still thirsty though, already his tongue was a little indiscreet. "But let me advise you," he implored dramatically.

Raoul looked at his friend kindly. "Go ahead. But make it snappy and do not repeat yourself, for any 'old-hat' stuff bores me."

"You have changed. I can see how it is with you," Georges told him earnestly, hanging on to the lapel of his friend's jacket. "It is your voice — your looks — everything. You are more alert — more human. Of course you are in love. It had to come to you. I am glad it is Caroline who has made the trick for she is a marvellous girl, so lovely, adorable and *chic*. Don't deny it, for I won't believe you."

Raoul was smiling no longer. He stood upright now, no longer leaning on the bar counter. "This is interesting." he said and urged: "Go on, Georges. A little more to drink and you will be quite illuminating."

Georges grinned fatuously. "Where was I? Oh, I know. Well, do not treat the passion of your lifetime as an experience which must have an end. If you do not make it permanent quickly it will hurt you both emotionally. Get going." He said a lot more which was irrelevant and Raoul listened with half his mind and in some amusement. He saw that Georges' glass was empty, and signified to the barman to repeat the order. Then he asked curiously, "Who told you to tell me all this, Georges?"

"Life!"

"Nonsense. It is Fanny. I do not say she told you to use such high-flown language, but she sent you to find out, didn't she?"

"Well, yes. She wants the best for Caroline."

"And I am Fanny's idea of the best. It is yours and Fanny's wish that I should fall for Caroline May? It does not matter much what she wants or I feel."

Georges protested volubly. "It certainly does. It was my suggestion that you wanted shaking up emotionally. Caroline seems to have done it."

Raoul glanced at his wristwatch. "You mean well, Georges," he said kindly, but there was that in his voice that closed the subject. "I should advise you to leave me alone. I am older than you, and well able to manage my own affairs. Now I must leave you. I look forward to seeing you and Fanny tonight. *Au 'voir.*"

CHAPTER XII

Raoul had spoken the truth when he had told Georges that the restaurant was fully booked for dinner. After Georges had gone, when the restaurant was closing for the afternoon, Raoul discussed the position with Jean, who said he could not possibly squeeze in another table without causing discomfort to the guests. They were joined by Henri, who had a more adaptable mind than Jean, whose gregarious nature believed that the 'more they were together, the merrier they would be'. He liked Georges and wanted to please him.

It was Henri who suggested that as these two who wanted a table for tonight were friends of Mademoiselle May, they should sit at her table and the three could dine together.

At first Raoul would not listen to the plan, saying it could not be done.

"Where would Miss May sit?" he asked. "If she sits in her rightful place, from which she can best carry out her work for me, she must face the room. I do not forget that is why some clients have booked tables — not to taste our excellent cooking, or drink our fine wines — but solely to have an uninterrupted view of Miss Caroline May. To sit with her back to the room would be discourteous to my clients, unsociable and unforgivable. There would be many real complaints. It could not be permitted. But, if Miss May faces the room as it is her duty to me and my guests to do, then she is also being rude to one of my guests who must sit with her back to the room. I do not doubt that Miss Cornell would notice the omission at once, and complain. Your idea, Henri, is therefore unworkable. You do not seem able to understand that Miss May is here to work for me, not to dine with her friends. She is not my guest, but on duty here."

"But you like to please the guests, m'sieur. You could make a concession for once."

"Naturally, but I do not wish to start a precedent, for immediately many quick-witted clients would take advantage of it. Many men would object to dining in loneliness, and ask to sit at her table. If I refused I might lose valuable clients. So I should have to give in. It would mean that besides arranging for table accommodation, we should have queues waiting to sit at Miss May's table. It would be an embarrassing situation for everyone."

But Henri was resourceful. "Could it not be a *fête* day for mademoiselle?" he asked. "That could not happen again for a year. It would be an occasion…"

So it was arranged.

The bank of flowers that had partially screened Caroline from the diners was to be removed behind her table, against the glass screens.

Even Jean, when this was done, said that it was an improvement. "It is a veritable background of spring for ma'mselle. She will be seen to true advantage."

Raoul silently agreed. By now he knew that the staff, with the single exception of Nini, adored Caroline. She seemed to have raised the spirits of everyone who worked at 'Maintenon'. They had been happy enough before, but her coming appeared to give them a new exciting zest for life. It was not so much what she said to them, but she smiled often, the slow, wistful smile of youth which they all noted and loved. Also, her gay looks and bright colouring fascinated them. Everyone went out of his way to anticipate her slightest want.

Raoul spoke to Caroline as she left the restaurant that afternoon.

Since that first night, when he had missed her, and she had gone off with Dale, Raoul had made a point of saying a casual '*au revoir*' to her. It required some ingenuity on his part to do so without making her suspicious that she was being watched. Also Caroline liked to slip away unobserved. Though she longed to see Raoul often she was still shy of him, and his nearness confused her. She was afraid lest he should guess how she felt towards him. This made her seem unnatural when she answered any questions he asked.

He said, "You will come early this evening, Miss May?"

She paused, then said, "Do you mean, earlier than usual?"

"Please." Then he smiled. "You will dine later, not alone, but with your friends, Fanny and Georges."

Caroline seemed surprised but pleased. "Are they coming? I am so glad. Fanny is longing to see my new dress."

"And are you longing to see it, too?" he asked, and for a second, as he looked down at Caroline's animated face, his eyes were warm, glowing and soft.

"Oh, yes."

He caught some of her enthusiasm. "So am I." Then he thought, *She is so sweet and defenceless against me, though she does not know it.* He thought, too: *It is dangerous for me to stay near her. If I do I may end in making such a fool of myself as to outclass Georges' tomfoolery.*

Caroline was thinking, too. She could not forgo the grooming which was her ritual before going to 'Maintenon' in the evening. It would be more important than ever tonight because she was to wear a new dress. Yet that would take time. It meant that she would have to miss the languages' lecture at the Sorbonne, for there was not time to return to the apartment after the lecture. This would be the third lecture missed within a week. At first Caroline's conscience had been troubled, but today it troubled her no longer. Apart from the fact that she was wearing a glorious new dress, there was an added attraction for the evening. Raoul had asked her specially to come early.

It had been an enjoyable day, and it was not ended yet. There was more pleasure to come.

The old clerk had been easy to work with. He had been full of compliments about Caroline and her work, telling her that he did not know how the restaurant managed to be so popular without her help. That was exaggerated of course. He had praised openly, simply and without embarrassment, saying what he would have done if he had been forty years younger, and wondering what the younger generation was about not to fall flat before her.

Then, too, Nini was not there to frown upon everything she did. It was tiring never to be able to do anything right. Even M'sieur Pierre seemed to feel the change in the atmosphere for he had unbent and smiled, and even joked with her.

Now Raoul waited to say, "Perhaps you would like someone to help you dress?"

It was a good idea, and Caroline thought of Louise who she knew was her friend, and who would like to see the new dress and she said: "Thank you, m'sieur. May Louise be here if I should need help?"

The enchantment of the morning spread to the evening.

It had been a lovely spring day. There was warmth and a promise of summer in the sun. Some of the larger, more-sheltered and enterprising of the cafes had placed rows of little marble-topped tables and chairs on the pavement, just outside their huge plate-glass windows, and had been well-patronized by patrons who liked to bask in the sun. Some patrons, of course, preferred still to sit in the bay behind the windows, and watch the passers-by through glass. There was plenty of life and gaiety on the boulevards.

Caroline would have liked to linger, because she loved the lightness, the reckless air that seemed to abound in the streets in spring.

The chestnut-seller was not patronized, but many people bought bunches of jonquils and mimosa, and even the big '*magasins*' were full of light-coloured spring clothes. Because Caroline was in love, and Raoul had smiled softly at her and spoken so kindly, she trod as though on air.

The apartment was empty, and instead of resting, which was a necessity if she wished to appear at her best in the evening, Caroline went over to the window which was open, and sat on the ledge thinking how beautiful the city was basking in the afternoon sunshine, with a slight blue haze in the atmosphere over the roof-tops.

The canary in the cage on the wall below her window sang cheerily because he liked blue skies and yellow sunshine, and glancing down to look at his cage, Caroline saw that the Prunus bloomed a mass of bluish-pink.

For a long while Caroline sat there enjoying the beauty and richness about her, her mind dwelling tenderly on love.

She was cramped from sitting in one position so long when Fanny came in.

"Hullo, honey, you are in early," she cried at sight of Caroline. "No lecture?"

"I didn't go. There was no time." Caroline stood up and stretched herself luxuriously.

"Well, I told you your days would be pretty crowded, and something would have to go. Did you know that Georges and I are going to 'Maintenon' tonight?"

"Yes, M'sieur Pierre told me. Am I glad, Fanny!"

"Oh, he's unbent that much, has he?" said Fanny, who knew every word that had passed between Georges and Raoul in the morning.

"He is never stiff — only aloof, sometimes." Then she asked, "How did Georges manage it?"

"He just wangled it. Georges has a way with him."

"He must be clever, for I heard Jean turning people away at midday." Then she added: "You are both to sit at my table. It is the only thing they could arrange at such short notice."

"That will be fun. I like a crowd. Aren't you terribly excited about your new dress?"

"I am dying to see it."

"And to wear it?"

"Of course."

But Caroline knew that half her pleasure in the dress was because Raoul shared her excitement.

True to her promise Caroline arrived at the 'Maintenon' in time to dress early.

Jean waylaid her in the foyer, and asked her to put a note on m'sieur's desk in the office. He had done this before, and Caroline had been a willing messenger. It was no trouble for her to put a note on Raoul's desk, and there was always the hope that she might see him and exchange a few words with him, and so assuage for a short while the longing for him which was growing up within her heart these days. It made all the difference to her.

She knocked and waited for his sharp "*Entrez!*" before she went in.

He had not expected her so early and rewarded her desire to please with a quick smile. He took the note and thanked her, saying: "Come in when you are dressed, Miss May. I shall wait for you here."

Caroline's smile was radiant as she replied, "I may be a little time, m'sieur; it is such a special night with all my friends here to see me."

Raoul thought, *You will look wonderful, my beautiful darling.* But carefully he kept these endearments to himself. "Then you'd better run along," he said gaily, and picked up the list of names of people who had booked tables for tonight.

He looked over the top and watched Caroline go, then taking a pencil from his pocket, Raoul ticked off names of sufficient importance to be mentioned to the Press, putting a star beside those who were photogenic or wore marvellous clothes, so that Henri could direct the camera men to their tables without delay or fuss. It was not, of course, compulsory for anyone to have his photograph taken, but Raoul's experience was that most people liked the delicate compliment.

"Are you so and so? Then may I take your photograph for the Press? Please go on talking. Be natural — thank you."

Raoul had meant to tell Caroline that Fanny, Georges and herself would be the guests of the 'house' for dinner. Actually he would pay the bill out of his own pocket, but he would not mention that to Caroline for she had quaint ideas about accepting gifts from him. He liked her for that, but he had to use his ingenuity to keep certain facts from her.

Raoul was aware, too, that Georges was dining at the 'Maintenon' tonight from the kindest of motives, wanting to help him and Caroline to the heights of his own present sublime happiness with Fanny, and hoping to find out if Caroline was attracted to Kit Dale, or if there was any other man in her life.

He had been more than a little disturbed at the mention of Dale's name, but he had decided to keep an open mind until Georges reported on the matter.

Georges, however, was drawing but small pay at the French Foreign Office, and could not afford the prices charged at the 'Maintenon'. Raoul had decided to give Caroline a hint about this. Georges himself would be delighted to be told that everything was on the 'house'.

Raoul frowned now as his eyes swept carelessly down the list which Henri usually prepared from Jean's book. Only half his mind was thus occupied. The other half was with Caroline.

Something struck Raoul as familiar in the list. His eye had caught some name that struck a wrong note. The frown deepened. Then slowly, keeping his mind fixed on what he was doing, Raoul read through the list.

Nearly at the bottom Raoul knew what was wrong. There, typed clearly, was a name, 'Mr. Kit Dale'.

Raoul threw down the list in sudden anger. His mouth, which had been so soft and sensitive when Caroline was in the room, hardened to a thin line. He exclaimed "*Bon Dieu!*" and swiftly his mind jumped to a conclusion. It was driven by jealousy, and was the wrong one.

Caroline had said she must look her best for all her friends — she could not say all for two people. She had known Dale would be here tonight. They were always meeting in the passage. He had seen them himself. It would be natural for him to have mentioned it.

Raoul thought furiously: *He is not the type I want in my restaurant. He does not know how to spend money to advantage — even if he has it, which I doubt. I do not dress her up for his sake, to make her look beautiful as an angel for his eyes to gloat upon. I shall not permit it. Dale shall not be served in my restaurant…*

Raoul thought a great deal on these lines, his mind growing angrier and more confused with each passing moment. It did not help at all because, deep in his mind, Raoul was aware that he was saying the impossible. He could not pick and choose clients.

Dale must have booked the table days ago. He had every right to occupy it and dine there.

I shall never forgive Caroline, thought Raoul, and wished, with growing impatience, that she would hurry back so that he could tell her how angry he was with her.

Knowing nothing of what was happening in the office, Caroline had unpacked the dress-box marked '2'. Louise, who had come in answer to a telephone call from Raoul to help Caroline, shook out the folds of the dress.

At sight of the dress, both women, who had been talking amiably, were silent.

It was of golden *lamé*, absolutely plain, with no trimming on it. The bodice of the dress was high to the neck at the back, but with a low *décolletage* in front, and long tight-fitting sleeves. It appeared to be close fitting to the hips, then flaring to the ground with a short train. The only ornament, if it could be called such, was a row of tiny buttons covered with the material which fastened the dress at the back.

Louise touched the dress reverently. "*C'est magnifique!*" she exclaimed and added that it was fit for a princess.

Caroline did not speak. She felt speechless, partly because of the beauty of the dress, and also because she was to wear it. A revulsion of feeling swept over her. Lately, all her emotions seemed so charged with excitement. She wanted to laugh and talk, but she knew that once she started it would be a meaningless babble of sound.

She looked at Louise who seemed delighted.

"Are you not pleased, mademoiselle?"

Caroline had to answer. She took a deep steadying breath. "It is wonderful," she said softly; "but far too grand for me. I am afraid to wear it. Perhaps I had better let M'sieur Pierre see the dress before I spoil it by putting it on? There may be some mistake."

"You must not do that, mademoiselle. M'sieur prides himself on not making mistakes."

"Then you do it, Louise. I have noticed that m'sieur listens with respect to what you say."

Louise shook her head. "I would not dare. My age gives me certain privileges, but there is a limit to what m'sieur will take from me. After all, he would think, what can Louise possibly know about these model dresses? She does not know why I order them, though I have very good reason. And m'sieur would be right. Put it on, mademoiselle. There is plenty of time. We are early yet. If m'sieur should not approve, you can change into the one you wore last night."

Caroline hesitated. She looked longingly at the dress shimmering in a kind of aloof beauty under the lights of the chandelier, and she said regretfully: "I am sure m'sieur will not approve. Toinette has forgotten his express wish, that the dresses were not to be conspicuous."

"But do not forget that Toinette is a law unto herself. I doubt if she would take orders from m'sieur about her dresses, any more than m'sieur would permit Toinette to tell him how to run a restaurant. Put in on, mademoiselle. It is a veritable dream."

When she was dressed, Caroline felt almost afraid to look at herself in the glass. In spite of Louise's almost prayerful attitude, with her hands palm to palm, and exclaiming fulsomely, and the knowledge that she was looking her best, there was a kind of fear in Caroline's mind. She was frightened of the idea of expense, that m'sieur who could be lavish might think this dress too dear for her, unsuitable for his purpose.

But thinking on these lines got her nowhere. Caroline's spirit began to clamour for action. The sooner she heard his verdict the better for her peace of mind.

The red light had been blinking with a rapidity which showed that someone was growing impatient of being kept waiting, and Louise urged Caroline to hurry.

With mixed feelings of hope and despair, longing to wear the dress, but worried in case Raoul should think it expensive and unsuitable, Caroline, with lagging footsteps, went towards the office.

Caroline knocked at the door. There was the usual abrupt "*Entrez*". Caroline opened the door and went in. M'sieur was alone in the room.

Raoul was standing by the window in a characteristic attitude, but he spun round at her entry.

Caroline saw at once that the handsome face was marred by a frown, which did not augur well for her hopes.

But even as she looked, and Raoul stared at her, Caroline saw his expression change. He became still.

Then slowly his dark eyes swept over her slim figure moulded by the exquisite lame, from head to foot — and back again.

Their eyes met and held. Some deep emotion that no effort of his willpower could subdue, and which he could not control, glowed in his eyes which seemed to glitter.

Caroline stared back fascinated.

Without volition on her part, the strength of this inner spirit seemed to call up an answering emotion in Caroline. Moments passed in tense silence.

The idea came to her suddenly, out of nowhere, unless it was conveyed by the warm look in Raoul's eyes, *I mean something to him.*

The thought, though nebulous, turned her dizzy.

She tried to speak, to appear natural, but failed.

Presently the feeling passed, and she saw that he had moved closer to her. She heard herself asking breathlessly, "You do like it: don't you?"

It seemed a long while before Raoul spoke. His voice was soft, warm and sweet, full of those tones Caroline loved to hear in it. "Of course. What else did you expect me to think?"

His voice thrilled her. Caroline did not answer. She could not.

Raoul did not appear to notice her silence. He continued, speaking excitedly, his voice a little slurred, as though for a short while emotion had broken through his resolve to be calm. He said: "It is *chic* — just what I wanted. You look wonderful. Toinette knows what suits you."

Then he laughed boyishly, and for once Caroline had a glimpse of youthfulness in him which she had not known before. "I could think of a dozen marvellous adjectives, and even then not express a fraction of the admiration I feel."

His hands went out towards her, but he seemed quickly to think the better of it, for his arms fell to his sides.

Caroline noticed this. She sighed inwardly.

Raoul asked, "What is the matter?"

"Nothing's the matter. I am so glad you like the dress, and that I may wear it. When I first saw it I was afraid..." She stopped, afraid of offending him, and destroying the peace between them.

"Of what? Come, do not hesitate, for I must know."

Caroline regained her confidence, and said suddenly and boldly, "You won't be angry if I tell you?"

"No!" Raoul said, and then he added slowly: "You have got to understand this. I shall never be angry with you now; and that is from the heart."

Caroline let that pass... It was a statement full of meaning. She would recall it later and think it out.

"You might have thought this dress too grand for me," she told him.

He seemed surprised. "Too grand! Oh, my dear Miss May, nothing could be too grand for you with that colour hair." Raoul laughed shortly, knowing that what he said was understatement. "You do not know me very well as yet," he told her gently, and asked, "Was there anything else you were afraid of?"

"It is glorious material, but you might have thought it too showy."

"*Certainement!* It does catch the eye, like golden light. That is as it should be, for I wish you to be better dressed than any other woman in the restaurant tonight."

Caroline sighed with blissful contentment. "You have your wish. Everyone will be envious of me this evening."

"Naturally, for you will outshine them all. It did not occur to me that you might fail."

Raoul knew that it was unwise and indiscreet to parade Caroline in front of his patrons. It might be asking for trouble. He thought recklessly, *What do I care?* He said critically: "Something is missing. Your garment needs a final touch." Then he had a brainwave. "Wait a moment." He picked up the book of telephone numbers and ran his fingers down the names opposite them.

Then he picked up the receiver and dialled a number, and spoke rapidly and at length in French to Madame Toinette. Afterwards he rang up a florist. Caroline heard him ordering flowers, a spray of dark red roses with touches of mimosa to lighten the darkness of the flowers — 'always remembering that the theme is spring time'.

Caroline thought, *Nothing is too much trouble for him.*

She wondered, as she had done many times this week, why Raoul was taking so much trouble over her. It was not only his desire for perfection of detail, and that everything he put his hand to must succeed. Even she was aware that there was some special urge behind all this planning, some motive force.

Could it be...? But here Caroline refused to let her mind wander further. She had never been such a focus point of so much attention from a man before.

Then she remembered how he had looked at her some moments before, as though his mind were unleashed for a moment and she could see the beautiful thoughts in it, and at the recollection she became confused and agitated, pacing about the room and not knowing that she did so.

Caroline was recalled to the present by Raoul's voice. He had finished telephoning and was watching her with his head slightly on one side.

He was saying: "When you came here some days ago you were lacking in confidence. Now you have perfect poise. It is unbelievable that such a change could take place." Raoul was thinking, too: *What did I do with my life six nights ago, before I knew her? What should I do supposing she left me for someone else?*

He looked down at his desk and saw the list of diners under his hand, and remembrance came back like the sting of a serpent.

Raoul's expression changed, and he asked abruptly, hoping by his abruptness to surprise the truth from her, supposing she wished to keep it from him: "Did you know that Dale was dining here tonight?"

The suddenness of the question caught her off-guard, as it was meant to do.

Kit was so much out of Caroline's thoughts at that moment, it was only with difficulty she remembered him at all.

"Why do you ask?" she questioned.

"Did you?"

Caroline flushed at the arrogant question. She looked straight into Raoul's eyes, saying, "Kit mentioned it the other day, but I had forgotten it until you asked me just now."

There was a little silence between them. Caroline was aware of a tension that had sprung up. The room which had seemed so cosy and happy, so full of soft light and shadows, so sweet and magical because they were alone in it, had subtly changed.

Then Raoul spoke, slowly, sternly and deliberately, driven by the insane jealousy that filled him. "I do not believe you," he said fiercely, shattering all that was beautiful between them. "You have not forgotten. Do you think I do not know why you wish to look lovely tonight? You are anxious to wear this dress so that you may be desirable in his eyes — this Kit. Do you think I have been blind since you met him? Or that I have not known of those many sly meetings in passages and on the stairs, and goodness knows where outside the restaurant?" He paused for breath, then went on bitterly: "What do you take me for? Do you imagine I am content to sit back while he makes love to you? Or that I am willing to dress you for his delight? I wonder I do not tear the dress from you and let you go downstairs in rags."

Caroline stared at him aghast. The last thing she had expected was an outburst like this. She went a pace nearer to him, standing so close that she could see some amber specks in his brown eyes, something she had not known before. She was trembling with something more than rage. Did not this clever man guess that she wanted to be lovely in his eyes alone — for him? He was blind if he could not see how it was with her.

She cried sharply: "How dare you speak to me like that! I will not stay here to be insulted by you."

Raoul laughed. It was not a happy sound. "Is it an insult to say I do not believe you? Shall I pretend and say: 'My dear Miss May, I am blind and stupid. I do not know what is going on under my nose. I want you to fall for this Kit Dale. He is such a grand fellow?' Because I will not. I do not. I hate the fellow."

Light came suddenly to Caroline. It cooled her anger and warmed her heart. She felt soft and melting towards Raoul who looked so attractive and magnificent in his anger.

She walked away from Raoul, towards the window, where she looked out over the night-lit city. With a great effort she spoke one word. It burst from her lips, and to Raoul it sounded cold and demanding. "Why?"

"Why?" he repeated stupidly. "Why do I hate Dale? Because —" and then he stopped suddenly, and there was another long silence in the room.

Caroline turned to face him again. Her eyes were bright, and the soft mouth trembled as she asked gently and mischievously: "Can it be that m'sieur is jealous?"

Raoul turned his head. "Me! Jealous?" He shook his head. "Oh, no. Why should I be? There can be no comparison between Raoul Pierre and Kit Dale."

"None at all," Caroline agreed. "Then I can think of no good reason why you should want to tear this lovely dress to pieces so that I have to go down to dinner in rags."

She was smiling a little, and in spite of himself Raoul softened. His anger, so swift to rise, and equally quick to go, dwindled as he made a gesture with his hand.

"It was a figure of speech. I cannot destroy what does not belong to me but to my firm." Then he said: "Forgive me, Miss May. I permitted my annoyance to get the better of me." And to himself Raoul said, *I must be slipping to show my feelings so plainly.*

Caroline smiled easily. "All right," she agreed amiably, but she was longing to ask: "Then why have you dressed me up? For whose benefit?" But she dared not question him further.

There was a knock at the door, and one of the pages, who were on duty in the foyer, brought in a spray of dark red roses.

The florist had obeyed Raoul's order implicitly, for the few fluffy balls of mimosa gave a lightness like spring to the deep colouring of the roses. The spray was in a cellophane box which Raoul handed to Caroline.

"Please wear these." Then he added, with a grin, "These are not on the house, but from me."

There was a hunt for some pins and Caroline went out of the room to the *boudoir* to fetch some.

While she was gone Raoul opened the box, and taking out the flowers carried them swiftly to his lips. It was a sentimental action, but he was deeply moved. Then quickly and quietly he replaced the roses.

When Caroline returned he was seated at his desk reading the paper *Le Soir*.

He watched her pin the flowers on her corsage, and noted that the petals he had just kissed were caressing her soft skin. An almost uncontrollable desire to take this lovely girl in his arms swept over Raoul.

"Will that do?" she asked carelessly.

"*Ravissante*, Miss May!" And then he asked again, "Am I forgiven?"

Caroline could not look at him. She could only tell him with a pretence of lightness, "Of course."

But she felt strangely tired as though she had been through a great ordeal.

CHAPTER XIII

Raoul went down to the restaurant with Caroline.

"May I lead you in?" he asked, but the question was perfunctory because he had already made up his mind to do so.

There was a short pause before Caroline said, "If you like." She tried to speak quietly, but could not quite disguise the tremble in her voice.

Caroline made a triumphant entry.

There was a babel of sound in the restaurant as the lift doors opened and Raoul stepped out. He turned to Caroline and held out his hand.

Though the action was casual, Caroline was to remember the soft yet steely feel of those fingers for some time afterwards.

People turned their heads expectantly. There was a queer sibilant warning sound. Suddenly a silence fell on the room, and everyone looked at Caroline.

She came forward slowly, smiling a little, looking so feminine, the sheen of the *lamé* bathing her in light, her head held high, her extraordinary hair shining like burnished gold. She was trembling slightly at Raoul's nearness. But no one guessed it for his touch imparted to her a beautiful cool assurance which gave her the appearance of a polished and self-confident woman. With smiling, lovely graciousness Caroline stopped often in her progress towards her own table, where Fanny, in peacock blue, and Georges awaited her, the latter standing up as she approached.

Just when Caroline reached the table, and there was no longer any need of his support, Raoul pressed her fingers reassuringly before letting them go. Caroline felt suddenly happy and radiant. A storm of clapping broke out. Caroline, surprised and delighted, flushed with pleasure. She smiled at everyone. They were all her friends. At this moment life seemed perfect. Raoul greeted Fanny, and then Georges. He, too, appeared happy and content.

Jean pushed in Caroline's chair, moving it slightly from its prearranged position, so that guests had a full view of Caroline's face. Though Fanny's dress was *chic* and colourful, and came from a noted house, her personality was dwarfed, and she seemed only a foil to Caroline, who was flushed, excited and animated as she had never been before.

Raoul smiled across at Caroline, saying, "Don't let success go to your head, Miss May, but eat a good dinner, or Fanny will scold me." But his eyes lingered on Caroline as though, according to Fanny's thoughts, he would like to eat her.

He went away, and for a moment no one spoke. But two waiters came to serve them, bringing the large white menu cards printed in gold lettering. Georges read his card and spoke to the waiter. Fanny's eyes were round and troubled. "I didn't know it was to be like this," she said oddly.

"Like what?" asked Caroline, looking at the menu card but not reading it because her mind was full of Raoul.

Fanny waved her hand comprehensively. "Such a parade! Such a magnificent dress. The cost of it must be staggering. These flowers — the pomp and ceremony! It is like a first night, or an Embassy Ball, or the foyer at the Opera House during an interval. It is like a dream. Raoul has mistaken his vocation. He should be a showman."

Caroline laughed. Her excitement was more controlled now. "But I told you the first dress was like something out of the *Arabian Nights*, Fanny, though it is not so lovely as this."

"I didn't understand, honey. This has gotten me beat. You'd have to be a painter, and then some, to make me see this set up properly, and even then I'd think you were drawing on your imagination. I wonder what the third dress is like?" Then she added: "You seem a very different girl here from the one who shares my apartment. Someone has put a spell on you."

"I don't feel the same," admitted Caroline.

Georges had been studying the menu. He put it down for a moment to say: "The difference is in Raoul. I've never seen such a change in a man. You've bewitched him, Caroline. He is quite human."

Caroline felt suddenly happy, though why she could not say unless she thought that Raoul was no longer indifferent to her. She recalled with poignant clarity the look in Raoul's eyes when they met hers in the office this evening. Then she heard Fanny say, still with that odd unease in her tone, "You look pale, Caroline."

"A first appearance is rather an ordeal, and I am naturally shy," replied Caroline.

Georges said, "I expect she's hungry, poor girl," and he proceeded to order a lavish dinner starting with a *bisque écrevisse*, for which the restaurant was famous, some fillets of sole *Rouennese*, followed by veal cutlets *Maintenon*. He suggested Fanny's favourite sweet which was a *soufflé* ice cream with brandy to end the meal.

"How will that do?" he asked, when the choice was finally made and the waiters had withdrawn.

"It is like a *fête* day," said Caroline, and was nearer the mark than she realized.

While they were waiting for the soup to be served, talking in desultory fashion and looking about them at the other diners, many of whom were settling down to dinner again, Kit Dale came up to their table, and Caroline introduced him to her friends.

He was wearing a red carnation in the lapel of his dinner-jacket, and looked well-groomed and festive.

He made no secret of his admiration for Caroline. Indeed no one seemed to exist for him except Caroline. He praised her dress extravagantly, but he was clearly astonished at its beauty, wondering about the cost, and why Raoul Pierre was putting on such a show, glorifying Caroline. Though he was not very clever about many things, Kit had a shrewd idea of what money could buy. On her part, Caroline, not knowing if Raoul were watching this meeting and was annoyed, decided to be careful. Her manner was reserved, though that simply drew Kit on like a magnet.

When Georges, in his large, hospitable way, said: "Are you alone? Why don't you join us?" Caroline reminded him gently: "This is not like the other tables in the restaurant, Georges. It is a business-table — like a stage. You mustn't invite the audience on to the stage without M'sieur Pierre's consent."

Kit said quickly, "Don't, because he won't give it." Neither man liked the other, for there was Caroline in between them.

Georges would not agree. Perhaps he did not understand the emotional forces at work. "Raoul is the kindest-hearted of men. Sit down, m'sieur."

Kit appeared to hesitate. "What do you think, Caroline?" he inquired, but there was longing in his voice and his eyes.

"I say no," she said in a low tone. "It is not only you to consider, but the precedence your sitting here would make for others."

Fanny sided with Caroline. "She's right. There is no point in making Raoul jealous."

A short silence followed this remark. Then Caroline, with heightened colour, said: "Don't be silly, Fanny. Jealousy doesn't come into it. I do not forget my place here, that is all. I should hate M'sieur Pierre to think I did. If Kit sits here then a dozen more men will feel that they can."

Fanny was annoyed at being called silly. "Oh, well, have it your own way," she said huffily. But Caroline knew that Fanny's short temper was caused by some secret worry, and she wondered what it was, for Fanny was a sweet-tempered, amiable person as a rule.

As Kit moved obediently away he said, "Never mind, Caroline, we'll make a day of it together on Monday."

Raoul was passing the table, and overheard the remark.

He had seen Kit go up to Caroline's table, and had watched him for some moments. Moved by an impulse stronger than common sense, he had hurried across the restaurant towards them, his fingers itching to remove Kit forcibly from Caroline. He had overheard the words, and was at once confused with a rush of thoughts. So that was what they were arranging? What was there between them?

He saw, as through a blur, that Kit had moved off. Then unable to trust himself to speak easily and calmly, Raoul passed by the table and went through one of the service doors out of sight.

The soup was served. The dinner was eaten by Caroline as in a dream. She was aware of eating and drinking, a good white wine with '*Château Candide*' printed in old lettering on the label, which Georges said was made from grapes growing in the de la Fallière's vineyards which were now being run at a tremendous profit by Raoul's cousin. Georges did full justice to the wine and was very merry and bright, as he usually was after a couple of glasses of wine. While everything still had the aspect of a dream, and they were lingering over their coffee, Fanny voiced some of the fears that had been worrying her ever since she had seen Caroline walking towards her that evening.

She said, her blue eyes popping meaningly, "I am just wondering where all this is going to end?"

"I know," said Georges brightly. "I'll tell you afterwards."

Fanny was as indiscreet as Georges. "I can guess; but I won't. Even Caroline would hate the thought of domestic security after limelight like this. I never connected such splendour with Raoul's mind."

"Don't worry, it is all in the nature of an experiment. Raoul is used to trying out schemes."

Caroline looked alertly from one to the other. "What do you mean, Georges?"

"I don't know," he admitted, passing his hand across his hot forehead. "After a week or two of this game we shall begin to see how it is going to work out; and that's all I can tell you."

"Yes?" Caroline urged coldly, wondering what Georges was going to reveal.

"Failure would mean that Caroline's 'turn' would come off. A success might spell the same thing. You see..." Georges' voice dwindled to silence. There was so much to say but somehow his tongue would not utter the words. Also Fanny was frowning at him, warning him not to talk too much.

"What are you talking about?" Caroline asked again, and now she spoke directly to Fanny.

"About you, honey. We're as worried about your success as we would be over your failure."

"You should worry. It has nothing to do with you," said Caroline.

Fanny and Georges exchanged glances, and Caroline asked quickly and suspiciously: "Has it?"

"In a way," was the guarded answer.

"How?"

Fanny intervened hastily, "We got you the job, because you wanted to stay in Paris."

"I know," Caroline said comfortably; "and it is up to me to hold it."

"That's right," said Fanny.

"If you can," cried Georges. He was sober, but not quite himself, or else his good sense had been scattered by a little too much wine. He had been listening intently, and now suddenly Georges wanted to take the centre of the stage and hold Caroline's attention. He knew he could entertain her better than Fanny could. She would listen to him.

Georges knew by the way Caroline's grey eyes were turned inquiringly upon him that he had her full attention.

"Why shouldn't I?" she demanded clearly.

Fanny tried to explain carefully. "It all hinges on Raoul. He is the boss here. You see, it was Georges who persuaded Raoul to create this job for you, and manlike he can't forget the good turn he has done a pal."

"That was kind of Georges," said Caroline, frowning because she felt that there was more behind this news than she was aware of. "I appreciate all that, of course. But I don't see —"

"You've got it wrong, honey. Don't thank Georges any more. He did not do this for your sake. He did it for Raoul's," Fanny told her patiently.

"I — don't — understand."

"Oh, you know how it is when a man has been ill and is bored. Raoul was like that. He was convalescing after flu, and Georges happened in on him. Georges is a sentimental idiot and thought something should be done for a man bordering on being a perpetual bachelor. He suggested that Raoul should look you over, in the hope —"

"Yes?" as Fanny became incoherent under the stare of those cool grey eyes.

"Don't be dense, Caroline," said Fanny sharply, wishing that her tongue was not so facile tonight. "It is all rather a lark, really. Why, in the hope that Raoul would fall in love with you, of course."

It was out now. Fanny waited anxiously, not sure whether Caroline understood the fun of what she had been saying. There was tension in the atmosphere.

Caroline looked piteously from one to the other, hoping that Fanny or Georges would say it really was fun, and that they were playing a joke on her. But she knew from the way Georges nodded rhythmically, with a set, owlish grin on his face, that she was hearing the truth. For a few moments as the truth and its implications burst upon Caroline she felt numb with shock. Her pride was hurt. She felt humiliated. It was as though the bottom had dropped out of her world leaving her alone and ashamed.

"Didn't you guess?" Fanny asked presently. "Georges wanted to give Raoul an interest in life, and he thought of you."

Fanny's voice seemed to come from a long way off.

"No. How could I?" Caroline caught at her scattered wits. She heard herself saying coldly, "I had no idea M'sieur Pierre was looking me over like a horse, wondering if he might get a bargain in buying me."

"Now you are being nasty, Caroline. It wasn't a question of bargains and dollars, but love. We both hoped — well — Raoul needs a wife badly, and —"

Caroline took a deep breath. "I see," she said dully. "How amusing! Georges certainly has a fertile mind." Then, quite suddenly, Caroline began to laugh helplessly. "It never occurred to me that I was dealing with three clever people who liked playing practical jokes."

Georges said in an undertone to Fanny, "She's had too much to drink." He put his hand on Caroline's, which was resting on the tablecloth, in an effort to stop her laughter. "Don't, Caroline. We shall be attracting too much attention of the wrong sort. Raoul will be furious with me for making bad advertisement."

"Oh, don't be silly. You know I have scarcely drunk any wine. I am not laughing at you, but at myself. I really tried to please M'sieur Pierre, to make a go of my job because I thought it was genuine. But I need not have troubled. It is all arranged. M'sieur Pierre knows what he is about. It was an ingenious idea. I take off my hat to his genius — or I would if I were wearing one. I only wish you had told me what was going on, so that I could have warned you not to waste time on me. It would be useless for M'sieur Pierre to fall for me in any way. What he may feel is of no moment, because I am already in love with someone else. I am not free."

Both Georges and Fanny looked at Caroline in consternation.

"Not free!" Georges echoed, shifting his eyes angrily to Fanny's face, as though accusing her of tricking him.

Fanny shook her head helplessly. "You are only saying that," she cried. "I know all your boyfriends."

"Not this one," Caroline told her triumphantly. "You don't know everything."

"Who is he?" Fanny asked suddenly.

Caroline thought wildly: *Who can I say? What name can I use?* In her confusion she thought of making up a name, but one would not come to her mind.

Then, like a brilliant flash of light one dawned upon her consciousness, and Caroline said perfectly coldly, "It is Kit Dale."

The other two looked across at Kit. He met their glance and smiled and waved. It certainly seemed possible.

Caroline continued: "I'm sorry I can't do anything to please you about M'sieur Pierre. Even if I had known of his intentions I should have turned him down. He is definitely not my sort. I cannot stand a man who spends his life carping about details because he aims at an impossible perfection. It would soon get me down."

Fanny digested this. Caroline was composed. *If I worked here and had been given a dress like that to wear, I should have been over the moon*, she thought. *But Caroline is not like me.* And she said aloud, "It could be true."

"It *is* true," repeated Caroline, but she was afraid lest Fanny should doubt her word and ask Kit if it were true. "Didn't you hear me making a date with him for Monday?"

Fanny and Georges began to argue. Caroline did not listen. She felt tired, nauseated and disgusted. The joy of the evening had gone. She felt the need for all her courage. *It isn't over yet*, she thought; *there is more and worse to come when I have to face him.*

Fanny turned to her. "You are sly, Caroline. When do we congratulate him?"

"Oh, not yet," Caroline told her hurriedly; "nothing is arranged, or will be for ages." She knew they were thinking it a lie, well, let them go on doing so. They had had their fun. It was her turn now.

Georges seemed worried. "What are we going to say to Raoul?" he demanded. "We've eaten his food and drunk his wine, and now we have to throw a monkey-wrench into the complicated machinery of his future. What do you think I, his pal, feel like?"

Caroline shrugged. Her own pain was too bad for her to feel any sympathy with Georges. She said, almost callously: "I do not think M'sieur Pierre will take it much to heart. His pride may be hurt for a while because he is not preferred to the poor accountant; but as a man of the world he must understand."

"He is bound to feel slighted after he has done so much for you."

"I did not ask for it. I tried to do my best for him, too." Then she added indifferently, "Too bad!"

"He may think we have let him down," pursued Georges gloomily.

"Have you?"

"I haven't, but somebody has."

"Meaning me, I suppose. Well, as I said, whoever is to blame, he will soon get over it. Perhaps one day he may realize how wrongly and rudely he has treated me."

Georges was shocked. "Now you are being absurd," he cried, and said something in a whisper to Fanny about "always the perfidious Albion", and "It goes right down through the history of France."

Caroline did not care. Nothing seemed to matter anymore. The dream she had so foolishly indulged in was over. Her dress seemed silly, the glimmer of gold a mockery.

A gloominess would have settled like a cloud over the table, but it was broken by Henri, who came up anxiously and asked Caroline if the coffee was cold.

She took the hint, and exerted herself to act, to pretend a gaiety and recklessness which she did not feel. But her heart was like lead in her breast. The evening that had promised so well was happily nearly at an end. Just when Caroline's head was aching so that she felt sick, and she was thinking how impossible it was to carry on any longer, Henri came up to the table again, saying: "Monsieur would like to see you all in his office."

Henri was smiling broadly. He was well pleased with the success of the evening, and especially delighted with Caroline. It had been a 'full' house. Everybody had enjoyed it. What more could a man desire?

"Now?" asked Georges a little fearfully, not wanting to face Raoul until he had had time to digest Caroline's news, and to think up something which would soften the blow this would be to his friend.

Of course Raoul has fallen for Caroline good and hard, he thought. *He will not take this news quietly. He will fight for her if necessary.* Georges even allowed his imagination to run on wildly, wondering if Raoul would call Kit Dale 'out', and if he, Georges, would be asked to act as 'second'.

He squared his shoulders, aware that Fanny was staring at him curiously, and not liking to seem afraid to face Raoul. He had dined and wined like an epicure, and after such a feast Georges did not want to repay Raoul's hospitality with bad news. He recalled that Roul had invited him to dinner for one purpose, to be reassured about his position with Caroline. So this summons, through Henri, could only mean one thing. Somehow, Georges was to 'deliver the goods', to tell Raoul what he wished to hear.

Georges sighed lugubriously. "Let's get it over," he said to Fanny, who was curious to see what Raoul's sanctum looked like. She rose with alacrity.

Caroline had not Georges' courage. She felt it impossible to face Raoul. She felt hurt and tired. She asked them to excuse her for she had a terrible headache and would like to change at once and go home.

Fanny said that was unthinkable, and the two girls rose.

"Don't leave us," implored Georges, hoping he could stave off any awkward questions and explanations. If only he could postpone this talk until tomorrow, when he had slept on the matter, or until it was daylight, when matters might take on a more hopeful aspect!

Fanny took Caroline's arm. "You can't desert us. It isn't our fault you happen to like Kit Dale," she said. "It's your business and so there's nothing to be said about it, but you must believe we thought we were doing something grand for you both."

The three went up in the brocade and gilt lift, which made two journeys to take them to the top floor, quietly, without speaking further. It appeared as though all the joyousness and hilarity that had marked the evening as memorable and enjoyable was a sham. There was, indeed, a kind of cold detachment about Caroline. The dress that had served to add to the lustre of her hair and make her such an attractive figure of life and light, a magnet for all eyes, now made her look cold, aloof and withdrawn.

Fanny saw the lines of pain in Caroline's face, and was moved to say: "Is your head bad, honey?"

"Terribly." But it was not only Caroline's head that ached until it seemed at bursting point, but her heart which lay quivering and wounded in her breast.

Raoul was in the office waiting for them. He looked at them with a sweet smile of welcome.

In spite of her hurt pride, and her anger against him, Caroline's heart missed a beat when she saw him standing against the ornate French mantelpiece, looking handsome and distinguished as usual. She could not bear to look at him, but turned her eyes away. She felt sick with misery, disappointment and disillusionment.

There were a magnum of champagne and several glasses on a tray on his desk, and a huge blue Sèvres china cigarette box.

Raoul drew up chairs for them, saying: "I was so sorry to break up your party, but it was getting late, and my staff want to get home. I believe you would have waited until the last client left, but that was not at all necessary. Now we can relax for a short while."

He opened the champagne, saying conversationally, "I hope you had a pleasant evening?"

With unusual and hurried *empressement* Georges assured him that the entire evening had been wonderful.

"That is what I thought," agreed Raoul, pouring out the champagne. "I heard many compliments about you, Miss May. One nightclub manager asked me if you were available for his cabaret. He suggested you might like to name your own figure to appear in it; but I said you were not an actress, neither were you free, and that money as such had no special attraction for you. I hope I did right?"

"Quite," Caroline managed to say.

Raoul must have thought her answer inadequate, for he glanced sharply at her, and Fanny rushed into the breach saying: "Caroline has a headache."

Raoul was at once full of concern. "Oh, I am so sorry." He picked up a glass of champagne and handed it to her saying, "Drink this, it will make you feel better."

"Thank you, m'sieur." Caroline took the glass and drank a little of the wine. "I'm all right," she said.

Raoul looked at Fanny, who shook her head dolefully.

"You are not like yourself, Miss May, so I shall believe Fanny that you have a headache."

Caroline did not answer. She sat there looking like an automaton and, until she had drunk two full glasses of champagne, saying nothing. Then she talked brilliantly and spasmodically.

Raoul was in good spirits. He drank little champagne, but smoked several cigarettes quickly, and Georges' heavy manner passed unnoticed.

Then suddenly Caroline rose. She could stand the situation no longer; and at once the two men got to their feet.

"I will go and change, m'sieur. It is getting late," she said quietly.

"Don't be long. We'll wait for you. I shall see you both home," said Georges.

"The car is waiting. Use that."

"No," Georges cried almost violently. "We have taken too much of your hospitality this evening. I shall get a taxi."

"You'll find it difficult at this time of night in this part. Do take the big car." Raoul spoke quietly, but he was puzzled at Georges' vehement manner. Usually Georges was only too ready and willing to accept anything from anyone, so long as he was not called upon to pay.

"No," repeated Georges loudly. He was chagrined to see that Fanny had jumped up with alacrity, saying to Caroline: "I will go with you and help you take that dress off."

"Please don't. I can manage." For Caroline wanted to be alone, to get a grip on herself.

Fanny insisted. She wanted to see the *boudoir* of which Caroline had often spoken. She was also anxious to leave Georges with Raoul, for she did not wish to be drawn into any discussion about Caroline.

When the girls had gone from the room there was a long silence. Raoul lit another cigarette. He did not sit down but walked over to the window and looked out at the darkened roof-tops, and observed the glow that hung over the centre of Paris, which would be there until dawn.

Georges did not speak. He stared moodily into space, wishing with all his might that Fanny would return and save him from the unpleasantness that was to come.

At last Raoul spoke. His voice was sweet and mellow as usual, but a little tired.

"I gather from your manner, Georges, that you have nothing pleasant to tell me?"

For answer Georges sighed deeply.

"Well, I am glad to know. At least the knowledge will save me from making a fool of myself."

"Caroline is not free, Raoul."

There was a sharp exclamation, then a long silence.

Georges looked away from his friend.

At last Raoul said, "Did she say so?"

"Yes." Then Georges said miserably, "I would have given anything not to tell you, Raoul."

"Why? It is right I should know."

"I am so sorry," Georges told him.

"So am I."

That was all.

Presently the two girls came back. Caroline was in her street clothes. She was quiet and pale. Raoul came forward to meet them.

"I can see that Miss May has still a bad head. I insist that you use the car, Georges." And to Caroline, who was looking forlorn and tired, Raoul said kindly: "If you do not feel better tomorrow, Miss May, please do not trouble to come."

"I shall be all right," Caroline told him briefly.

Raoul went downstairs with them, and out through the staff entrance where the big car was waiting, the chauffeur sitting stolidly at the wheel.

He opened the car door and helped them into the car, bidding them *au revoir* and standing in the yard until the car had turned into the main street.

Raoul returned to his office. It was full of her presence. He glanced about the room, his thoughts wretched. If Georges had not given the one reason, Raoul would have put up a fight to win Caroline, but without love he could do nothing. Without love he did not want her. Then he went over to the mantelpiece and leaning his arms on the marble shelf he bent his head to the shelter of his arms. A groan burst from Raoul's lips.

"Oh, *mon Dieu*! How shall I bear it! *Mon Dieu*!" he cried out in agony.

CHAPTER XIV

The following day Caroline turned up at the 'Maintenon' as usual.

She met Raoul, who asked, "Is your head better today, Miss May?"

"I am quite well, thank you, m'sieur." That was not true for Caroline's head was no better.

They had both slept on their misery of heart, but while Caroline's spirit had hardened against Raoul, he was full of perplexing questions that must be answered before he could accept Georges' opinion. Last night Raoul had felt too stunned to understand fully the position. It was different today.

The two avoided each other during the day. Caroline was glad for she felt she could not bear to meet Raoul often. She wanted to cry but she must not give way to emotion.

On his part Raoul began to wonder why Caroline was so anxious to avoid him. Her attitude puzzled him. He could not force his company upon her in the restaurant. There were too many ways of avoiding him; also it was too public. Yet he must see Caroline alone before the restaurant closed or he would get no rest.

That evening, Caroline wore the black and gold dress which she had christened Number One. Raoul noticed it but made no comment. In any case he could not expect her to live up to the concert-pitch state of the previous night. There was bound to be reaction.

Caroline did not see Raoul to say 'goodnight', and made no effort to find him. Her one idea was to get back to the apartment and tell herself she was the most miserable girl in Paris, and perhaps cry herself luxuriously to sleep.

She ran down to the staff entrance, to the car which stood as usual in front of the sporting car which belonged to Raoul Pierre and in which he usually drove home. The chauffeur was not in the big car, and while Caroline stared nonplussed, not knowing what to do, a familiar voice spoke to her from the shadows of the sports model.

Raoul said: "This happens to be Emile's night off. I shall run you home in my car."

"Please don't trouble. It is early and I can take the last Metro."

"It is no trouble." Raoul opened the door on the off-side. "Please get in."

"No, thank you. I would rather —"

"Get in," Raoul ordered sharply. "If you do not get in quickly I shall put you in."

Still Caroline hesitated because giving in to him might seem a sign of weakness. Then she appeared to think better of it, or perhaps she knew that Raoul was capable of carrying out his threat, for she got into the small car.

Raoul stretched an arm across her to shut the door.

It was a wide seat, large enough for three people to sit in comfort, but Caroline squashed herself into a corner, leaving a space between them.

Raoul did not speak, but drove off quickly and even recklessly, over the bridge and across Paris.

Before turning into the rue Tino, Raoul stopped under an archway, where it was dark and silent. Caroline looked at him questioningly, and he said quietly, "I want to talk to you." He moved nearer to her.

"I have nothing to say to you," Caroline told him frigidly.

"Why not? What has changed you since yesterday? You are not yourself. What have I done?"

Why could he not leave her alone? Caroline refused to be drawn into explanations, so she said: "Nothing."

"That is nonsense. It is not like you to treat a man unkindly for nothing." There was no answer and Raoul said softly, as though speaking to himself: "If I am to be punished I may as well do something to deserve it... I might kiss you, then you could box my ears."

That drew an answer as Raoul expected it would.

"Please," said Caroline, stiff with fright in case Raoul carried out his threat and she would not be able to hide the yearning for him that was in her heart. "You must not talk to me like that. Drive on."

"Oh, no, not until you have explained."

"There is nothing to explain."

"I agree, but somehow that does not mend matters between us." Gently he put a hand over hers which were folded over the bag in her lap. For a few moments hers fluttered under his firm touch, and then were still.

The gesture — or rather, her reply to his gesture — made Raoul feel tender towards her.

"What is it, Caroline?" Raoul asked caressingly, and was not aware that he spoke the name which was so often in his head.

But Caroline heard it and never had her name sounded so poignantly sweet in her ears.

His touch no less than his voice went straight to her heart, but she dared not show any emotion, in fear of weakening.

She pushed him away, saying sharply, "Don't."

Raoul took his hand away and Caroline shivered as with cold and wished she had not been so quick to reject the warmth.

Raoul did not move back into his own seat, but remained disturbingly close.

He said confidingly, "You know, it is I who should be terribly angry."

"What for?" she was surprised into asking.

"Because I have been cheated. When I gave you your job I thought you were free. Georges told me last night you are not. I am angry. I have every right to be."

So he knew. Caroline was glad. The knowledge closed every door between them. Caroline hoped it would make him understand the unbridgeable space that separated them.

She said coldly, "I can understand how you feel because you like to be first, m'sieur."

Raoul shrugged. "I should have liked to be first with you. With anyone else I would not care."

"What am I supposed to say to that?"

"Just tell me if Georges spoke the truth. I want to hear from your own lips that you are in love with another man, and then I shall have to believe."

There was a long silence. Thoughts hammered and clamoured in Caroline's tired brain.

"That is easy," she told him with an attempt at bravery, but in spite of her efforts her lips trembled ominously. "I am in love."

The words sounded odd, halting and shrill. Raoul's lover's ear heard the falseness of them.

"Oh! You are in love. Just like that. It is morning, or night, or sunny, or raining. 'I am in love.'"

Caroline caught her under lip in her teeth. She thought wildly, *It is true; I am in love.*

"Do I know him?" Raoul asked presently.

"Yes. It is Kit Dale." She spoke challengingly.

"Ah! So soon! You have but known him since you met me."

"Well, what of it? That is how love comes — suddenly," she told him defiantly.

Raoul reminded her gently, "We are discussing love, not carrots in the market." Then he added: "Perhaps you are right. But don't forget I was first. I might point out that I went slowly so that you would not be frightened and put off me, because my love is not like yours. It is tempestuous, passionate, adoring. We should not think we were talking about the weather or carrots, where my love is concerned." He paused, then continued in a different tone: "Someone not cursed with my fears stepped in ahead of me — and he won. That was unfair of Fate."

He turned his head to look at her face, a white wedge in the half-light, hoping to read something from its expression. He felt baffled, but why he could not say, for Caroline had made the position plain enough. Just then a car passed, and by its lights Raoul saw her face — tortured, pale and miserable. She did not look like a girl in love, but so young and unhappy, so much in need of comforting that his heart went out to her.

He forgot she was inimical to him. He only knew she needed love.

Involuntarily, swiftly and surely, giving her no time to repulse him even had she wished to do so, Raoul raised his arm, and putting it around Caroline's shoulders, drew her closer to him in the friendliest way.

"*Chérie!*" he whispered, and put his cheek against hers. "*Ma p'tite chérie!*"

At first Caroline's natural impulse was to repulse him, then she became still, for there was no mistaking the genuine love-note in his mellow voice. She had a sudden strange longing to relax in his strong arms, and to forget Georges' indiscreet remarks which had shattered her happiness; and she had a yearning to recover the lost ground and be friendly once again with this man.

While she was thinking thus, Raoul turned his face to hers, and holding her tightly to him kissed her on the lips.

Caroline stirred strangely. She had never been kissed like this before — so gently, and yet with such passion and strength. She had not known that such endearing and caressing words existed, or that any man would feel the need of saying them to her — the slurred dar-r-r-ling! *Chérie*! *Mignonne*! Such lovely sounds!

Caroline knew somewhat hazily that after what had happened she should repulse Raoul. She wanted to do so, but somehow his kisses had taken away her power to do so. She was governed by her emotions. She tried to push him away, but he was not to be gainsaid.

Suddenly something in Caroline gave way to him. She could fight against him no longer. His kisses satisfied some hunger within her, a hunger she had not been aware of until lately. She was swept away on a tide of passion the strength of which Caroline had never thought any human being was capable of feeling. Then thought became confused — and then she ceased to think...

It was Raoul who came to his senses first. He released her slowly, like a man awakening from a beautiful dream he is loath to lose, his cheek pressed against hers once more, and then he gave a last kiss on her hair.

"Coppermob," he said affectionately.

He sat back in his seat, and used both hands in a sweeping movement over his head from his temples to the nape of his neck, as though he would clear his mind of those cloying and confusing thoughts which emotion had aroused in his brain.

He spoke thickly and tiredly with the strain of his emotions. "I suppose I must say I am sorry," he told her. "I have to be because you are in love with another man. It was wrong of me to let myself go like that. But I lost my head. You did, too. So we must both feel terribly sorry and agree never to do such a thing again. I shall not — unless you ask me, which is most unlikely."

Caroline did not answer, but Raoul did not expect her to. What could she say?

Caroline had fumbled in her bag for her powder compact, and was busy repairing the ravages which Raoul's hot kisses had caused to her face. She worked intently in silence.

Raoul watched her, a queer light in his eyes.

"Let me see?" he said gravely when she had finished and was putting away the compact.

Obediently Caroline turned her face towards him for his inspection, but she would not look in his eyes, but at some point beyond his head.

"It is a nice face," Raoul told her softly at last.

Raoul did not linger, but before he started the engine, he said casually: "It is my free day tomorrow, too. Will you give me the pleasure of dining with me? I know a nice little place in the Bois, where the food is epicurean. There is still so much I have to say to you. I am sure, if I keep strictly to business, that Dale will not mind your dining with me."

"I am sorry, but —" Caroline was beginning, when Raoul interrupted.

"Of course. The other fellow! He got in first there, too. I must be losing my nerve or something. I am not usually so slow and careful when I want something badly. This happened to be important and I did not want to spoil things by rushing my fences. What about making a date for the following Monday?"

"Perhaps," stalled Caroline. "It is a long time off."

When Caroline got in the apartment was empty, for Fanny was spending the weekend at her aunt's flat. Caroline's emotions were still so mixed and strained that without waiting to take off her hat and coat she flung herself down on her bed and began to cry. She had been a schoolgirl when she had enjoyed her last good cry. Now it was as though all the pent-up emotions of the last ten days were pouring out of her.

She wept copiously. There was nothing and nobody to stop her. Caroline forgot everyone in the exquisite relief of floods of tears. She cried on and off for hours. Actually she had no clear idea why she was crying — unless it was that everything had combined to ruin her happiness.

She had been excited about her work, the new clothes, and Raoul. Georges had spoiled her happiness. Fanny had overloaded her with advice. She was furious with Raoul, whom she had idolized, but whose feet had been proved to be of clay. No doubt, at this moment, Raoul Pierre was dying with laughter over the way she had clung to him and returned his kisses. At the crook of his little finger, her defences against him had crumbled. She had made a fool of herself for a few moments' tenuous happiness.

As a matter of fact, Raoul, driving home through deserted streets, had no thought of laughing at Caroline. Alone in his car, acutely aware of this lovely girl's presence, he was certain that Caroline did not love Dale. No girl could kiss a man as Caroline had just done if her heart and mind were given to another man. Obviously the affair with Dale was a mistake and would soon peter out.

During long wakeful hours in the night, his heart and mind still full of Caroline, Raoul was obliged to admit that she had not been entirely frank with him. There were times when he felt uneasy, jealous and angry about Dale who had the special pull over him of being Caroline's countryman.

Meanwhile Caroline wept. It was a long while before she even tried to regain control of herself. When at last she did so, Caroline rose wearily from the bed, removed her crumpled dress, bathed her swollen eyes, and made hot coffee.

She drank the coffee at the open window, and watched the dawn breaking through in the east.

Later, when Fanny returned, she exclaimed at Caroline's looks. "My, you look as though you've been on the roof all night."

"My head is splitting."

"Then stay in bed and have a rest. You need one badly."

"I must, for I can't get up."

It was arranged that Fanny should ring up Kit's office, and tell him that Caroline could not go out with him today.

Then Caroline fell asleep deeply for hours.

In the early evening she woke up feeling refreshed, with her headache gone, to find Fanny, in an overall, cooking their supper on the gas-ring.

"Better?" Fanny asked.

"I am feeling fine."

"I seem to be making a mess of this food. Shall we go out for a meal?"

"No, I don't want to go out. It'll be all right," said Caroline. The chill of reaction came over her again, but she must make the effort to hide her depression from Fanny.

It was when they had eaten supper that Fanny tried to satisfy her curiosity.

"Did you see Raoul yesterday?"

"Oh, yes," Caroline steeled herself to answer indifferently.

"What was he like?"

"All right: the same as usual."

That was disappointing. Fanny liked to hear something dramatic. She said: "That's odd, for Frenchmen don't usually sit back, and make no fight over their love affairs. Has he never made love to you?"

Caroline flushed vividly, but she answered casually, "A little."

Fanny said reflectively: "I am sure if you had encouraged him Raoul would be madly in love with you. It doesn't do to be too cold and stand-offish."

"Thanks."

"Not of course that you should set much store on a volatile Frenchman's love-making."

"You need not go out of your way to warn me," Caroline told Fanny tartly. She was not like Fanny, who loved talking publicly about emotions. "M'sieur Pierre is too sure of himself for my liking. He is always right. I think I hate him."

"Love or hate, it is the same thing. The dregs of boredom are reached with indifference." Then Fanny added inconsequently, "But I wish you had fallen for Raoul instead of Kit Dale."

"Why?"

Fanny shrugged. "More fun. You'd find Raoul more satisfactory. Frenchmen make love so nicely and expertly. They seem to be born with the knack of knowing how to love."

It was an exquisite torture for Caroline to hear this, but she replied grimly enough: "It needs experience to be expert. I imagine M'sieur Pierre has had many women in his life."

"How come?" and Fanny thought, *What a kid she is!*

"Did you see that photograph on M'sieur Pierre's desk the other night?" Caroline asked suddenly, and then she remembered that it was missing, for the tray of drinks had been put where the photograph usually stood.

"No."

"It was probably in a drawer." And Caroline thought, *Perhaps it was "off with the old love" before he kissed me.* A kind of bitterness came over her in a wave as she recalled her own weakness last night, and she thought too, *That shall never happen to me again.* But it had happened, and shown up her weakness.

"What is she like?" Fanny asked curiously.

"What you would expect: young and beautiful."

"She would be. I can promise you that Raoul Pierre's choice would be something exquisite. Trust a Frenchman for knowing what's 'tops'."

Then Fanny began to talk of something else. It was so obvious that Caroline was unhappy when she spoke of Raoul, and it was cruel pursuing a subject that brought such a crucified look to a girl's face.

CHAPTER XV

The following morning was a trying one at the 'Maintenon'.

Nini was back after her weekend, with the usual flood of plausible excuses about the chill that had kept her in bed through the weekend. Raoul scarcely troubled to listen, but told Nini not to bother him with trifles. That was in itself suspicious, and soon Nini was aware that they were well-founded. During her absence this new girl had somehow managed to push her, Nini, down in Raoul Pierre's estimation.

Of course Nini heard about Caroline's second success. Indeed, Louise, with childish delight, took pleasure in letting Nini know all the kind things people were saying about Caroline.

The first thing Nini did was to complain to Raoul about Caroline's mistakes with cash.

"She is an imbecile, that one, m'sieur," she ventured to say stormily.

Raoul turned on Nini at once. He had been trying to concentrate on work all the morning, but his mind was full of Caroline, whom he had not seen since saying '*au revoir*' to her in front of the janitor of her apartment house.

"Miss May is not a fool. Everyone says she is delightful and charming, but you," he defended.

Nini was taken aback by the ferocity of his tone. "They do not have to balance the cash, m'sieur. I should prefer it if mademoiselle did not take the cash-box from me. It is a responsibility I do not care for. Cannot M'sieur Henri do it?"

"I will ask him," was the unexpected reply. "Then you shall not be worried by Miss May anymore."

His cold voice stung Nini. She tried to draw someone else into the quarrel.

"M'sieur Dale did not come yesterday. I left out work I expected he would do."

Raoul snapped her up savagely, not because he cared a jot when Dale went through the accounts, but because he guessed that Dale's absence meant he was with Caroline.

I won't allow it, he told himself stormily. *I have no intention of standing aside, and letting Dale take my girl from me. What do they take me for?*

Raoul grew more restless, and waited in a fever of impatience for Caroline to arrive.

When Caroline appeared Raoul was waiting for her. His eyes searched her face closely, observing that she looked pale, and there were lilac rings about the lovely grey eyes.

Raoul's emotions were aroused at sight of her. Insanely, he wanted to take her again in his arms, and hold her close, to kiss her lovingly and passionately, to reassure himself that what had happened the other night was not a dream. He worshipped her. But he dared not show a flicker of feeling, for Caroline was at her coldest, disdainful and unapproachable, holding him metaphorically at arm's length.

Besides, Nini was watching their meeting, and her big, black, glistening eyes missed nothing.

So Raoul said in his most business-like tone, which matched Caroline's coldness: "Good morning, Miss May. Did you have a nice time yesterday?"

Caroline's eyes met his fleetingly. She was embarrassed at meeting Raoul. It is difficult to speak naturally to a man when his arms have been about you and you have exchanged fervent kisses, especially when you feel he has made a fool of you, and you have made an even bigger fool of yourself. A ghost of a smile crossed Caroline's face at Raoul's question.

"Quite."

That told him nothing, and Raoul asked again, "Did you go sightseeing with your friend?"

He must know if Dale and Caroline were together.

Caroline stared at him coolly. "No, m'sieur. I stayed in bed all day."

That sounded far-fetched, for Caroline did not look sick, and Raoul frowned.

"You were not ill, Miss May: or were you?"

"I had a headache, and I was tired," she replied briefly.

"Tired!" Raoul repeated. Had his love-making wearied her? Had she been bored?

But Caroline's mind was on another track. "I know you do not call it work for me here, but it is a strain being here and doing my own work. Going to bed so late every night does not suit me."

She sounded as if there was cause for a grievance, and in sudden panic Raoul wondered if this were the thin edge of the wedge and she was going to say she must leave him.

"I have never said you do not work. I do not think as you say," he told her quickly. Then he asked, "Must you go on with your art classes and languages?"

"That is the reason why I came to Paris."

"But the work here takes all your energy."

"I only work here at all that I may stay in Paris and pursue my studies. Without that reason I should return to England."

Raoul thought, *So she is making use of me*. And he said, "I am so sorry," just as though everything that was wrong about the job was his fault and he must take the blame. But he was really concerned about Caroline's tiredness, for he did not like to see her lovely eyes spoiled by shadows. He had no idea that Caroline had wept on his account, because of him.

He smiled gently and placatingly at her. "I must see what can be done about these late hours," he told her.

Caroline gave him no answering smile, but stared woodenly at him, waiting patiently for him to release her.

The week that followed was tiring and disagreeable. Nothing seemed to go right for Caroline. Kit Dale's work over the accounts progressed slowly. Waiting with ill-concealed impatience for Kit to finish and go, Raoul became suspicious and bad-tempered. There were many small scenes which made Caroline feel wretched. Not only had she to deal with Raoul but also with Kit, who seemed suddenly soured. Whenever he spoke of Raoul he added a bitter gibe.

Caroline listened mostly in silence, but there were times when she was forced to defend Raoul, and stop Kit's barbed tongue. The staff were invariably kind to her, but there again, Caroline was aware of a strange unrest which had something to do with herself though she could not put a name to it.

Nini was openly rude. That was to be expected, for she had a great admiration for Raoul, and was jealous of the approach of any other woman.

Then, on Friday, when Caroline's nerves were beginning to show the strain of late hours, and the continuous torture of being near Raoul, whose manner throughout the week had been impeccable, impersonal and cool towards her, something happened.

By accident on Caroline's part, and design on Kit's, she met him on the stairs, just around the corner of the passage.

"At last!" Kit cried triumphantly, seizing Caroline's arm, and swinging her about to face him. "I have waited for several days

203

to get you alone. I believe you have been avoiding me. Also the watch-dogs in the office seem to have conspired against me. But I knew if I waited long enough my chance would come, and it has. Now, don't fuss, because you aren't going to escape me easily without some explanation. You promised to go out with me last week, and you failed me, pretending to be ill. As if I believed that. You went out with Pierre."

Caroline's chin went up. Kit's familiar, hectoring tone, more than his words, annoyed her. She resented the way he held on to her arm with a heavy pomposity of manner, a kind of proprietorship over her which she had not noticed before.

"Let go of my arm," she cried sharply.

"Oh, no you don't. You'll be running away without answering, probably taking shelter in his office, as you have already done this week."

"If you don't I shall scream and make a scene," Caroline warned.

"Go ahead. It won't do you a bit of good. I can spin a good yarn, too."

Caroline knew she dared not scream. She was at Kit's mercy.

So she said resignedly: "Let go of my arm, and be quick then. What do you want? I suppose I've got to listen."

"Caroline!" Kit was hurt. He let go of her arm but remained alert lest she should prove too quick for him and outwit him.

That he was exacting and jealous was obvious. Kit knew he was showing himself to her in a bad light, but he could not help himself. He loved Caroline. She must see how it was with him.

He said resentfully, "You would not dare speak like that to *him*."

"Do you mean m'sieur?" Caroline inquired haughtily. "He would not dream of behaving so monstrously. He would know better."

"And I don't. There you go, taking his part. Can't you see it is wasted on him, Caroline? I beg of you not to burn yourself at his fire."

"That is my business."

Kit was stung to retort, "And mine."

"Oh! Why?"

"Because — I love you." There, it was out now, and Kit felt better. It would be plain to Caroline why he wanted to be with her, why he took such an interest in her and wanted only the best for her.

Caroline did not seem to take things Kit's way. She asked scornfully, "And do you think that gives you the right to be rude and hectoring to me?"

"Caroline, don't speak to me like that. Don't look at me so coldly." Kit shook her slightly. "Darling, what have I done or said that you should treat me like this…"

For answer Caroline looked at him steadily. She was thoroughly ashamed of Kit.

Something in her eyes abashed him. It was plain that she had no use for his love.

Kit was not sure whether at that moment he loved or hated Caroline.

He leaned towards her, his mind confused, longing to hurt her, yearning to kiss her soft lips, his hands itching to touch her.

He said in a thick voice, speaking like a drunken man who has an obstinate purpose of mind, yet is not able to convey his purpose, "There is one thing I will not allow you or any girl to do, and that is to make a fool of me." He realized that she was adamant.

Caroline was aware then that she could not reason with Kit. No one could. She shook her head helplessly, as though confessing that the situation was beyond her.

As she did so, Kit's arms closed around her like a vice. He drew her towards him, and roughly, without kindness, even without love, governed by passion, and feeling brutal to the girl who had scorned him, Kit bent his face to hers and kissed her fiercely.

It was at that moment Nini, also urged by the flame of jealousy that burned within her whenever she thought of Raoul and Caroline, and in search of them, saw Caroline in a man's arms. It was not Raoul but Kit. Her swift Gallic mind switched to this new chance to depose a hated rival from favour. It was Nini's moment of triumph.

She rushed to the lift to find Raoul. As she did so the door opened and he came out.

"*Vite*, m'sieur!" Nini whispered to him. "Those two — on the staircase — hugging — kissing!"

Raoul understood, the situation at once. It was as though he had been waiting for and fearing this.

Shocked, outraged and goaded by Nini's wild words, he ran swiftly and quietly to the staircase.

Then he stopped.

As Nini had said, Kit and Caroline were there!

But they were not locked in each other's arms and kissing passionately as Nini had said and Raoul's imagination visualized. He understood it all at once in the passing of a moment. It was like looking at a swiftly moving picture which is presented dramatically to the sight, and in a flash has gone.

Caroline was in the act of boxing Kit's ears soundly. She was white with rage.

Raoul withdrew. They were both far too much occupied with each other to look up and see him. He had an impulse to confront Dale, but wisdom prevailed, for instinct told him that Caroline had the matter under control.

Nini was waiting, her eyes questioning.

Raoul's expression hardened. He spoke sharply to her. "Get back to your work, and mind your own business."

Raoul did not wait to see Nini go, but walked into the lift again and went down. He felt better than he had done for days.

Caroline did not know what was happening about Monday, her free day, and whether she would be going out with Raoul or not. At first she scouted the idea that she would go with him even if he begged her to do so. She had decided in her mind how she would answer him when he repeated the invitation. It only remained for Raoul to speak.

But Raoul said nothing, and presently Caroline found herself giving him chances to ask her out, making it easier for him, in case he was suffering from her first rebuff, to suggest a meeting.

Still Raoul was silent, and Caroline grew anxious, worried in case he had accepted her first refusal, or forgotten that he had invited her. She even contemplated giving him a hint, but decided that he might think that impertinent, or humiliate her by saying that he had now made other arrangements.

Then, when she had resigned herself to staying in the apartment, perhaps in bed, Fate smiled again.

It happened on the Sunday that Fanny said casually to Caroline: "My aunt has asked me to take you along to her flat for a drink this afternoon. She has read about you in the social columns of newspapers and wants to meet you."

Caroline did not want to go. She was not in a mood to make herself attractive to Mrs. Cornell's guests, the sort who would expect her to be as entertaining as she had to be at the 'Maintenon'.

She replied, "That is very kind of Mrs. Cornell, but —"

"Have you a date?" Fanny asked.

"No."

"Then you are going for I won't take no. It isn't good for you to be mooning about here all by yourself. It will do you good to get out and mix with people. What you need is a froth-and-bubble party. Be ready at five o'clock. That will give you an hour there."

Caroline gave in because it was too much trouble to argue with Fanny. Also, she thought it would not do her any harm to go.

Perhaps Fanny is right, she thought, *and it will do me good to go.*

Mrs. Cornell's *salon* was crowded with Americans and French people. She was a large woman and wore a large hat. She looked large-hearted; and welcomed Caroline with both hands outstretched to her.

"I have heard so much about you from Fanny. Let me take one good long look at you." She studied Caroline's face closely. "You are exactly as Fanny said, except that she did not say enough."

Mrs. Cornell at once introduced all the people around her to Caroline, who was soon the centre of a throng of people who seemed eager to know her.

Caroline entered into the spirit of the party. She had a couple of cocktails and felt exhilarated, and began to talk and laugh with animation, so that the press of people about her was great.

Caroline's confidence returned under the flattery showered upon her. She knew that she would not find peace and contentment anywhere until she had found it within herself. Soon she was feeling young and gay once more, and if there was a maggot of unhappiness deep within her heart no one guessed at its existence. It was a lovely room, decorated and furnished with French antiques, and the gilt of the furniture of a bygone gay age had mellowed with the years, and gave an air of luxury and magnificence, and even a little sadness to the present age.

It was easy, too, to hide the unhappiness which Raoul was causing her under an armour of bright trivialities, for everyone around her appeared to be enjoying life.

In the middle of her gaiety Caroline was aware that Raoul Pierre had entered the salon.

Her roving eyes had caught sight of someone bending over Mrs. Cornell's plump hand — a dark, sleek head that looked so familiar Caroline glanced back twice. In a sudden rush of joy she knew who it was. Her heart, which had seemed so heavy and bruised, leaped in her breast. In a moment she had forgotten every vestige of her depression, and felt as gay as she sounded. Though still talking to some men around her, Caroline knew presently that he had left Mrs. Cornell and was looking about the room as though seeking someone.

At the same time Caroline was aware of a feeling of astonishment that it had not occurred to her how admirably Fanny, and possibly Mrs. Cornell, had arranged this meeting.

Then she saw him standing on the edge of the crowd about her, a sweet familiar smile widening his sensitive mouth and lighting up his eyes.

He raised his hand and waved gaily as he caught her eyes.

"Hullo!" he cried.

Caroline could only guess at the word. She could not hear his voice in the din about her, but because she was so delighted at seeing him so unexpectedly, Caroline found herself smiling too.

At the same time that queer sense of unreality that had seemed to cloud everything she thought and said lately, when with Raoul, returned in full force. Everything about Caroline seemed unreal, the people mere puppets. There was a buzzing in her head. She saw Raoul as through a haze. Though the room was packed with people, all extracting the maximum enjoyment from the scene, Caroline had a strange feeling of isolation. She was in a world alone with Raoul Pierre. No one else counted.

Such was the power of Raoul's personality, the crowd between them seemed to part to make way for him to pass towards her.

As he took her hand, bowed over it, and swept his lips lightly on her knuckles, Caroline noticed, what she had not observed before, that Raoul was wearing, on the edge of the lapel of his black jacket, the unobtrusive little red ribbon of the *Légion d'honneur*. She wondered what service he had done for France to win that, and her heart swelled with pride in him.

In a kind of enchantment she saw him raise his head and look at her, still holding her hand in his, and say: "It is so hot in here. Shall we go into the ante-room where the crowd is thinner, where we can talk about two special things that are in my mind?"

It was like being wrapped in happiness to hear his mellow voice speaking to her, urging her to come into another room so that, away from the din, noise and fuss, and the constant interruptions, he could talk to her. Then she was suddenly curious of what he wanted to say.

Caroline told herself not to be a fool a second time, but to assert her independence and refuse to go. But seeing Raoul so unexpectedly, and finding him so friendly after the irritations between them during the week, was enchanting, and she found herself eager to go with him and to hear what he wanted to talk about.

Anyhow, Caroline was beyond reasoning with her emotions just then.

So they went into the ante-room, which was a narrow strip of a room between the *salon* and the *salle-à-manger*. People were continually passing through the double doors of both rooms, passing across the ante-room to do so. But no one bothered much about those who sat on a long gilt stool, covered in faded Genoese velvet, placed across the window. Perhaps they guessed the two would wish to be left alone

As they seated themselves, a servant brought them some drinks. When he had gone they did not speak for some moments, then Raoul, who had been looking at her profile for some minutes, said: "I get so few chances of speaking to you alone. It is impossible at the 'Maintenon' where the atmosphere is so business-like. What with conferences and telephone calls, not to speak of orders, complaints, and other business details with people who feel they have a right to my time and attention, I could not get to know you as I should like. Here, they will let us alone."

Caroline did not answer because there was nothing to say.

They finished their drinks, and Raoul put the glasses on the base of a bronze statue.

Then Caroline looked at him and said, "You asked Mrs. Cornell to invite me here today?"

"Yes: do you mind, Caroline?"

She flushed at the sound of her name, and said simply, "I am glad."

They sat relaxed and happy.

Then Caroline stirred lazily, and asked almost absently, "Why did you especially wish to see me today?"

"Why?" Raoul echoed in the same tone. Then he exerted himself to say, in that melodious voice which Caroline had come to love, "First of all, I want to tell you how desolated I am not to be able to take you home tonight."

Caroline's face, which a moment ago had been so soft with happiness, now froze. The lovely spell between them was shattered.

It was only now, when Raoul told her so plainly there was to be no repetition of last Sunday's madness, when his arms had been about her, and they had kissed each other so passionately, that Caroline realized how much she had longed for Raoul to do the same thing again.

The satisfaction of that night had been short-lived. She was not content now with a few kisses; but wanted something more. This refusal to repeat it — and Raoul's words were tantamount to that — meant he did not want to kiss her again. Her kisses had meant nothing more to him than a pleasant interlude.

Caroline felt hurt and humiliated. Even in her wretchedness she thought miserably: *I asked for this by leaving the party to sit with him. What is the matter with me? Must I always behave like a fool?* Why could she not grasp how foolish it was to reach out for the unattainable? It only meant more hurt.

She hugged the remnants of her pride together, and heard herself say distantly, without any warmth or challenge in her voice: "I did not expect you to, m'sieur. I can easily take the

Metro. Now that I no longer do the cash with Nini, I have plenty of time to catch the last train."

Caroline thought wildly: *This must be the first act in telling me to go. He has told Henri to do the day's accounts with Nini, so that I can go home by train.*

Raoul seemed to take no notice of what she said, but continued: "Emile, as you know, goes off on Sunday. I have an important conference with my chef."

A conference, thought Caroline swiftly, *The businessman's excuse to avoid doing something he does not wish to do. I know all about such conferences.*

"And so I have arranged with Emile's son, Louis, to drive you home."

That was kind of him, but Caroline said in a dull voice, "You should not have troubled, m'sieur."

"It is no trouble."

Caroline did not answer, but thought again: *I will not be ordered about like this. I shall not use the car. I will go by train.* And she thought too, *That is number one off his mind. Now for the other news.* Obviously there would be no arrangements for meeting tomorrow.

Mentally, she steeled herself to hear it.

The silence seemed to weigh heavily in the air. On Caroline's part it was not one of content or understanding. Then suddenly, without warning, Raoul moved his hand, resting it lightly on Caroline's, which were folded tightly together in her lap.

She moved restlessly, her mind in a dither, not knowing what to make of this move on his part.

Raoul leaned towards her saying so softly that without knowing it, her fretted nerves were soothed, "We are friends, Caroline?"

There was an assurance in the question, as though he could not believe they could be otherwise than friendly. He only wanted her to say so.

Her first impulse was to reject him, to push away his disturbing personality, and refuse to listen to the honeyed words. But something within her stopped Caroline from acting on that impulse, and she said lamely instead, "I suppose so."

He removed his hand at once, and Caroline felt cold and shivered.

"You only suppose," he said haughtily. "Either we are friends or we are not. There must be no half way in friendship. I must have a plain answer, yes or no."

As she did not reply immediately, Raoul ordered: "Look at me. That is better. No matter what your voice says to me, it is your eyes that speak the truth... That is better," as she raised her grey eyes unwillingly to meet his. "You do like me a little, Caroline?"

She could not meet his eyes for long, but looked down, only to raise her eyes a moment later, and say insolently, "Is it so important that you should know, m'sieur?"

Raoul hesitated. Then he softened, and said gravely, "It is, because liking implies trust."

"Well, as you have asked me, I do not trust you," she said flatly, remembering what Georges had repeated about his talk with Raoul Pierre which had led to her being offered the job at the 'Maintenon'; and how Raoul had made love to her a week ago, not because he had any love for her, but to amuse himself in an idle moment.

"I am sorry," Raoul said after a while; "but I think I shall tell you what is in my mind, and let you judge for yourself what I am asking of you, and how far you may trust yourself with me. Please relax while I explain."

Caroline waited in silence, aware, just now, that Raoul was going to say something important, aware, too, that silence might be her valuable ally.

Raoul spoke, gently and quietly, with no trace of that arrogance he had shown a moment ago. He wanted her to understand what he was saying.

He said: "It is my free day tomorrow, and I want to make the most of it. That is why I am so busy tonight, in preparation for my being away all day tomorrow. Usually I go to my office for a couple of hours on Monday to see that everything shall run smoothly while I am absent, but there will be no time tomorrow."

He paused and saw that Caroline was listening attentively, her forehead puckered a little with thought or distress, he could not tell which.

Then he went on: "I have planned to go to see my mother tomorrow. It is two hours by air to the nearest airfield to the Château Candide, and then an hour's motor run across country. If I start early I can have *déjeuner* with my parents, take a stroll in the pinewoods of which I am so very fond, and return to Paris in time for dinner."

Caroline nodded to show that she was listening. Only once had Raoul Pierre mentioned his mother, and that because she happened to telephone when she, Caroline, was in the office.

She was thinking: *He is spending the day with his parents. He is going a long way to see them. Why is he telling me this? Perhaps he is going to ask me to dine with him on his return. But I won't do that. I can't. I want something more than that from him, which he cannot give to me. I must be strong and refuse, for to be that kind of friend to him will only hurt me.*

She was aware then that Raoul had moved closer to her, and his voice had dropped to a seductive and thrilling whisper, so that she had to bend close to him to hear what he was saying.

"Now I am coming to the great favour that I must ask you, Caroline. Will you come with me tomorrow?"

At first Caroline thought that she had not heard aright; then she imagined he was joking. It had not occurred to her that Raoul would wish her to go with him.

Caroline turned her head, and looked wide-eyed at him, astonishment and even consternation on her face. Was she dreaming? Then, when she understood the full import of his words, Caroline shook her head decidedly.

"Go with you!" she exclaimed stupidly and awkwardly. "Why should I?"

"Why not?" he countered quickly. "I shall promise to take great care of you. I shall behave most beautifully. You shall see."

Caroline felt breathless. Her heart was beating fast, and her cheeks were flushed. She repeated mechanically, like a doll that had been wound up, "But why, m'sieur?"

"It is simple. Because I have told my mother all about you, and she wishes to meet you. I, too, want you to know her. She is not able to travel to Paris just now, and so we must go to see her."

Dizziness and confusion were in Caroline's mind. She could not think clearly.

Raoul meant it! He wanted her to be with him all day!

Caroline was afraid of saying anything quickly, in case she said the wrong thing. She was unwilling to make a decision, too, because that odd feeling of unreality was upon her again, and she was afraid of making a mistake as she had done before. But more than anything she was afraid of being hurt by him.

She could take it from Kit or any other person, but not from Raoul.

Her fear must have communicated itself to him, for he pleaded: "Please, do not say no. It is so important that you should go with me to see my parents."

They looked into each other's eyes, and Caroline was enchanted by what she saw, and she said slowly and softly, as though the words were drawn from her in spite of herself: "I will go with you."

His eyes danced with pleasure.

"*Chérie*," he cried. "I knew you would come." Impulsively he took both her hands in his, raised them to his lips and kissed them hard.

Then he held them from him, opened his hands and looked down on them, white and small, lying crumpled and still in his palms.

"Such little hands!" he whispered; "but oh, what power is in them!" Laughter crept into his voice as he saw her expression, and he said: "I shall tell you tomorrow. We shall laugh at it together."

A servant approached Raoul, reminding him of the time. Raoul looked frowningly at his wristwatch. "*Bon Dieu*! I had no idea it was so late. That fellow is like an alarm clock. I must go. You must go, too. I shall give you a lift. Shall we go together to say *au revoir* to Mrs. Cornell?"

CHAPTER XVI

When Caroline told her friend that she was going to fly to the Château Candide with Raoul, in the morning, Fanny said: "So it was Raoul after all. I knew it was, and that you were only kidding me about Kit Dale."

Caroline looked purposely blank. "I don't know what you mean."

Fanny laughed good-naturedly. She had known long ago that Caroline was reserved. "You don't have to think it out, honey, I am not surprised at your news. Matrimony in France is a family affair. In many ways it's a swell idea, but it gives so little loophole for escape supposing one changes one's mind."

That had not occurred to Caroline. She had been looking at the matter from the English angle, but Fanny's cryptic words made her so excited that she could not sleep. Caroline told herself that Fanny was imaginative and indulged in wishful thinking, and it would be silly to pin any faith in them; and to a certain extent Caroline succeeded in controlling her emotions. Raoul had never said anything to make her dream dreams. She must be reasonable or this lovely friendship would be spoiled.

In the morning, in spite of lack of proper sleep, Caroline looked more beautiful than ever. She was lovely, radiant and vital when Raoul called for her at eight o'clock in a taxi.

Even the janitor, who had finished his morning's work and was reading his daily newspaper in his little box of an office by the open front door, noticed the change in Caroline. He had never been known to joke with anyone, but this morning he said to Raoul: "It is unbelievable, m'sieur, what the spring does to people, even getting them up early."

Then he raised his bushy eyebrows resignedly as someone in a room above began to practise singing.

"Do-re-me-fa-fa-fa-fa — la, la, la."

"As early as the larks," he added somewhat grimly.

Raoul was in holiday mood. He brought a spray of freesias for Caroline, saying, "This is a festive day, and flowers always play a big part in festivity."

He watched her with soft eyes as Caroline pinned them on to the lapel of her coat.

"Do I look nice?" she inquired, smilingly, when she had done so.

Raoul did not look at the flowers, but at her face.

"You look enchanting, but then you always do."

Caroline flushed and thought: *There is no one so nice as this man. I am lucky to know him.*

They walked across the courtyard to the taxi which was waiting in the rue Tino.

There was a dazzling quality in the air this morning. They both felt it, and glanced around them, at the houses around the courtyard. A man was hanging out his bird cage, and the bird began to sing at once. There was a girl, half-dressed, hanging some bits of washing from a pole stuck out of her window. The blossom on the tree in the centre of the courtyard was dying, but the sprouting leaves glowed green in the early morning sunshine.

Fanny leaned out of the top window of the house, her blonde hair gleaming in the sun.

Even the dust-cart, which entered the courtyard as Raoul and Caroline left, looked romantic.

There was a small *contretemps* at the airport, when an official wished to put a large dress-box, which Raoul had brought with him, among the baggage in the 'hold' of the aeroplane.

"I shall put it on the rack," decided Raoul, rescuing it from the crate of cases.

"It is too large, and will fall on someone's head, m'sieur."

"Then I shall tie it on."

The official seemed about to begin an argument, when Raoul took him aside and spoke to him in a low voice.

The man glanced slyly at Caroline who was waiting to walk up the gangway to the plane.

He began to laugh. "*Oh, oui, m'sieur. Oui, oui. Je comprend, trés bien.*"

Not only did he carry the box into the plane, but tied it securely to the rack, and was well rewarded by Raoul. Caroline noticed that it was one of Toinette's dress-boxes, and she thought idly either that Raoul was acting messenger for his mother, or he was taking her a present.

There were other passengers in the plane. Visibility was good, and when they were airborne, Raoul leant across Caroline, and pointed out all the notable landmarks of Paris and its environs.

He was an agreeable companion, not sharp and nervy as he was in his office at the 'Maintenon'. Caroline was enchanted with his manners, his voice — everything about him, or was it because she was in love, the sun was shining, she had started on an adventure, and was determined that everything today must be perfect?

Of course, everything might be different tomorrow, thought Caroline. The carping spirit, and the jealousy that had seemed to beset Raoul, might be back and he would find fault with everything she did, and discover that people had complained, and she had not reported it. He might call her slow in acquiring the experience necessary for her job.

But tomorrow was another day. Caroline was determined to make the most of this one, and to extract all the goodness and loveliness from it.

Raoul was at ease. "Time does not exist for us today," he told her blithely. "If we are not back in Paris in time for dinner, we will go to a nightclub for a meal. There is one, the Rose Blanche, over in St. Germaine where I should like to take you."

The prospect sounded delightful.

At the airfield they were met by a large, old-fashioned car; and were driven through lovely countryside bordered with poplars, where every inch of ground was cultivated by hardworking peasants, and small red-roofed cottages, like dolls' houses, dotted the landscape.

They drove through pinewoods, where the air was redolent with a tangy freshness that exhilarated Caroline, so that she felt as though she were drinking wine.

Then out of the pinewoods, through a valley, fed by a narrow lively river which seemed to talk as it rippled over a stony bed.

Around a bend, at the head of the valley, on a knoll was the gabled and turreted Château Candide, gleaming white in the spring sunshine.

At sight of it, Caroline, who had been chattering excitedly, grew suddenly silent.

It was not so much the size of the Château, or that it stood as a memorial of the ancient glories of a bygone age, but the fact that it belonged to Raoul's family, and would belong to him one day. It was a symbol of the distance between them.

In Paris she had grown accustomed to his good manners and simple outlook. They had understood each other. Now

Caroline knew it was impossible to know each other ever. Their upbringing was so different, hers in the poor country parsonage with a number of brothers and sisters, and his as a member of this old family.

Raoul said anxiously: "Why are you so quiet? Don't you like it?"

"Oh, yes, it is beautiful — like a museum piece," she said in a small voice.

"It is more than that. It is a home."

Caroline thought, *Your home.*

They drove along the sheltered valley. On the sunny side, on terraces, planted in neat rows, were thousands of small bare bushes, and Caroline asked, "Are these your vineyards?"

"Yes, my cousin runs them for me."

"I know. Georges told me."

"Oh, Georges seems to have repeated quite a lot about me," he said half-vexedly.

"That is because he is proud of your achievements."

The car swept through the open ornamental wrought-iron gates of the park.

And so to the Château.

Raoul looked sideways at Caroline and told her reassuringly: "Do not look so pale and frightened. My parents will love you for yourself, though they have a great admiration for the English as they will tell you at once. Besides, I am with you."

Caroline smiled at him softly. He was so understanding.

At the top of a low wide flight of steps the Marquis de la Fallière was waiting for them. He was a tall, thin old man, wearing a black skull-cap on his bald head, and a large rug around his shoulders.

As he welcomed Caroline, his deep-set, hawk-like dark eyes looked closely at her. He spoke in English. It was not so good as his son's.

He took them indoors, through a vast marble hall to a wing of the Château, into a small high room with a painted ceiling and painted panels to the doors. It was richly furnished with tapestries and French *marqueterie*, tulipwood and kingwood furniture.

The Marquise, in a heliotrope dress and ermine *paletot*, was sitting in a *fauteuil* beside a log fire. She was a tiny, faded old lady, looking like a piece of rare porcelain, and had a white poodle sitting on a footstool at her feet. Caroline saw a faint resemblance to Louise, only the latter suffered by comparison as a coarse imitation.

She, too, was delighted to welcome Caroline. After a few minutes' talk she took Caroline's arm with a friendly gesture, and led her upstairs to tidy up after the journey. All the time the Marquise talked of her adored Raoul, not knowing that she was draining away all Caroline's confidence, and increasing the distance even more effectually between Caroline and Raoul than the Château had done.

She asked, "What part of England do you come from, Miss May?"

"Norfolk. My father has a living near the mud flats of the Wash. It is bleak and cold, much different from this place."

"Oh!" the old lady exclaimed. "How odd! I know Norfolk. My husband's great, great, great-grandfather was rescued from the Revolutionary hordes by the English, and taken to Norfolk. We went there for our honeymoon. I love the English."

Caroline's heart warmed towards her.

Paris seemed a long way off. Indeed, the world outside the Château Candide appeared to have no existence. Caroline saw how easy it was to forget the world in this lovely old place. One could eat, drink and sleep. It might be fine or wet — but only as a kind of background in a dream.

Caroline took a long time combing her hair and powdering her face. There was so much to see and enjoy in the little room. She allowed herself to drift into the haze of peace that cloaked the house.

But at the back of her mind, though she refused to admit it then, Caroline knew there was a world — her world — to which she must return at the end of this perfect day.

Other members of the family joined them for *déjeuner*, Raoul's cousin and his wife, and several enchanting children, and the parents of the cousin and his wife, and a couple of nephews, and distant connections in the ramifications of French family life, all of whom were acknowledged and accepted in the pattern of life at the Château Candide.

Everybody was kind and attentive to Caroline, who sat between the Marquis and Raoul.

They are treating me like a princess, she thought, and smiled often.

They drank champagne for *déjeuner* as a matter of course. The grapes were grown on the estate, and the wine was distilled at Bordeaux, where the de la Fallières owned a large company and exported vast quantities of their wines.

In the middle of the meal, one of the cousins asked Raoul, "What is this trouble with your chef at the 'Maintenon', Raoul?"

He laughed lightly, as though the matter were of little consequence. "It is an unusual trouble. The chef feels that his art is unappreciated by the new clients who have swamped the place lately. You see, they are more interested in seeing

Caroline than in eating epicurean food. That is natural, for they are a young crowd and have yet to learn the science of eating well."

The cousin did not take the matter so lightly as Raoul had done, and said unsmilingly but with good practical sense: "Mademoiselle has started a war of cooking versus beauty. With all your fine nose for detail, Raoul, I bet you did not consider that angle."

"No, it was new to me," admitted Raoul.

"I should not let the chef go if you can help it. Without him your receipts would fall."

"Undoubtedly. I think the trouble shall settle itself soon."

"*Bon.* After all the hard work you have put into the restaurant it would be a pity if the business fell apart so easily."

Until then, Caroline had been enjoying her *déjeuner*. The food was good but delicate, though she liked such food. But after listening to this talk about the chef, aware that her presence at the 'Maintenon' was doing harm to Raoul, she felt wretched. Raoul had known of this and had said nothing to her about it. If anything was to be done it was up to her. She would clear out, and the 'Maintenon' would quickly settle to working in the old way with the chef's art of paramount importance. No one need be distracted from food by a smart girl in a Toinette dress.

It would mean the end of everything for her, for she would not have the heart to remain in France any longer. She would return to England, find a job of some sort in London, and do the sensible thing — forget Raoul. It was a sickening thought, but there was no use in fighting against the power of the chef who could make or break Raoul's livelihood.

"You are not eating, mademoiselle," said the Marquis in some concern.

And Raoul asked: "Is anything the matter, Caroline? You look so white."

"She is tired," said the Marquis kindly.

"No, I am not a bit tired… How can I be when the air here is like wine?"

Raoul said: "After *déjeuner* we will go for a walk in the pinewoods. They are so restful. You will like that."

Caroline thought, *We shall take a walk but there will be no rest for me, for I must tell him that I shall be leaving "Maintenon" at once, never to return.*

When *déjeuner* was over, Caroline sat on a stone seat on the terrace, and talked for a while to Raoul's mother.

"Sit close beside me," said the Marquise, "where I can see you."

She took Caroline's hand in her own frail one, and said slowly and quietly: "I am so glad that Raoul brought you here to see us today. We have heard so much about you both from him, on the telephone each day; and also through the gossip-writers. No one has over-praised you. It has been a great pleasure to us to meet you, though I have no doubt you have felt it a strain meeting so many people of one family at once. Though we all admire you, we must have been also a little critical, for we love Raoul, and think only the best girl is good enough to be his friend. We have found you good and simple as well as lovely, and Raoul is a lucky man. This, of course, is only a beginning, and I hope soon we shall see you again, and as often as you care to come."

Caroline was touched, but there was sadness in her happiness for she knew that this would be the last time she would see these nice people.

She said a little tremulously: "That is very kind of you, madame. You will spoil me if you say such nice things about me. I shall get swollen-headed."

"I do not believe it. You are not that sort of girl."

Raoul had been walking up and down the terrace, smoking and talking to his father.

Now he came up to his mother and Caroline and asked, smilingly, "What secrets are you two talking?"

"No secrets, but what everyone in Paris is saying about Miss May, that she is charming."

Raoul nodded and said, "That is so." Then he said quickly to Caroline, "Shall we take a little walk?"

"Please." But Caroline shivered, for she felt cold suddenly. She had already decided what must be done, and was reluctant to have to do it.

Raoul kissed his mother '*au 'voir*', and whispered, "I may have a surprise for you before I go."

"What is it?" she asked, for she was at an age to take a childish delight in surprises.

"Ah, that would be telling."

It was easy to see that Raoul adored his mother. He was so gentle with her.

"Come on, Caroline," he invited urgently, and there was that in his voice which brought the hot colour to the girl's cheeks.

Once out of sight of the terrace, Raoul linked Caroline's arm in his, entwining his fingers in hers.

They walked swiftly towards the shelter of the pinewoods, their feet making a crackling sound on last year's bracken, and paused time and again to look through the tree trunks to the sunlit valley. The silence between them grew tense.

Presently Raoul said, "Shall we sit for a while on this fallen tree?" and he loosened his fingers from hers.

"Yes." Caroline felt like fainting. Almost she wished it were possible to pass out so that she need not tell Raoul she would never see him again after tonight. She wondered, too, if she would have the strength to be so ruthless with herself.

They sat down on the fallen pine and said nothing for a while.

Raoul stole a look at Caroline. Her eyes were closed, and there was a look of suffering on her face which frightened and baffled him for he had not the key to her thoughts, and wondered what was in her mind.

He said, "Do you like this?"

Caroline roused herself to say: "Oh, yes, it is a lovely spot. I can hear a lark singing as it rises into the sky."

"Then why do you not look at it, *chérie*?" he inquired with unusual gentleness.

Caroline opened her eyes, and Raoul saw that they were misted with tears.

"Dar-r-r-ling, what is it?" he pleaded, putting his hand momentarily on her wrist.

Oh, the heart-tearing tones in his voice! Caroline wished he would speak to her harshly, for that would harden her spirit, and make her feel less grieved at parting with him. But he had not, and the sound of his voice made her want to run away and hide, so that she could cry luxuriously alone.

When she spoke it was in a strangled kind of voice. "Had your conference with the chef last night anything to do with me?"

Raoul paused and looked at her searchingly, then turned his head and gazed at the dancing river winding like a ribbon along the floor of the valley.

He said quietly, "Yes, it had."

"Why didn't you tell me?"

"I did not wish to worry you."

"But it concerned me."

"Of course, but you might have been disappointed."

"What did you say to him? I have a right to know."

Raoul hesitated again, as though not sure what or how much to say. Then he said boldly: "I told Chef you were leaving the 'Maintenon'; that after today you would not be returning. I also added that within nine days the restaurant would be on its old footing, and your name, which hit the headlines with such a bang, forgotten."

There was a silence after this blunt outburst.

"You said all that?" asked Caroline breathlessly, feeling angry but helpless at such cavalier treatment. Yet that was the sort of blow she had been preparing to deal him. But she told herself passionately that it was not for the same reason.

Then as the true significance of the words struck her, Caroline shrank away from him.

"And more," Raoul said loudly. "It pleased Chef, for he is above all things practical."

Caroline winced. "Oh!" she cried faintly. "You did not think to consult my wishes."

"No. I should have done so soon, but Chef forced my hand."

"I see." Words were futile now, but Caroline felt she had to keep her end up, and pretend a little longer. "So it is you who have chosen to write '*finis*' to my job which has been such a spectacular success and an abject failure, m'sieur. I might have guessed you would be the one to hurt me."

Caroline tried to speak jauntily, as though she did not care, but the result was a miserable failure, for her mouth quivered and she could not hide it from him. How could he be so cruel! If he had to tell her that she was no longer wanted, surely he could have done so quietly in Paris, and not brought her here for a showdown? At the same time, in her heart, Caroline knew there must be some mistake, for Raoul was not cruel.

He watched her without speaking for a while, and then he said plaintively: "When are you going to stop calling me that ridiculous 'm'sieur', Caroline? I thought we were friends. When shall I hear you say 'Raoul'?"

Caroline looked at him strangely and flashed, "Do you think I could be friends with you after this?"

"*Mais, oui*. It was a business matter. Our friendship is apart from business. Why not?"

"Why not, indeed," Caroline echoed with a bitterness new to her. Then she added wearily: "Oh, have it your own way, I don't mind. We can be anything you like until I go home to England, I suppose," and she thought, *What does anything matter now?*

Raoul came close to her. He slipped his arm about her waist, holding her forcefully to him.

"But I shall not permit you to go home to England, Caroline. *Bon Dieu*! I have not gone through a torture of jealousy for two weeks but to let you run away from me in the end. You have lost your job at the 'Maintenon', but I have a much nicer one to offer you in exchange."

Caroline pushed him angrily from her, and rose to her feet.

"I don't want to hear what it is. I won't take it. I, too, have had as much as I can bear from you. I am going back to England to forget."

Raoul had jumped to his feet. "No," he cried in a ringing voice that brooked no argument. "You shall never go. Why do you think I brought you here today?"

"I neither know nor care now. I am through with everything to do with you."

"You may be. But I insist that you shall listen to what I have to say first." Then his voice changed subtly, and she was aware that his gentle tones were stealing into her heart, softening it. He said: "I wanted you to meet my people, Caroline; and I wished for them to see you. I so much wanted you to like one another. I longed for you to see my home and where I lived in the hope that you would love it as I do. I hoped, more than anything, that you and my mother would take to each other.

"Even if you think I have behaved badly to you, and you are angry, you must believe me, Caroline."

By the depth of his voice Caroline could tell how much Raoul loved his mother, and she said quickly: "Well, you've had your wish. You should be happy. We did take to each other — so what?"

Caroline was at bay now, a little defiant, on the defensive, unsure of herself. Raoul was 'getting at her' through his mother. It was unfair. He had all the advantages at his call.

Then he shrugged, saying whimsically, "Even if you had not, if all my relatives and friends had hated you at sight; and if you had not liked my home, or the country life, it would have made no difference to me really.

"When Georges urged me to meet you, to make a job for you in my restaurant so that I might get to know you before giving away my heart, I knew that Fate had something big in store for me which might change the whole course of my life. I tried to stop it, in my own way, but it was of no use, for it was something larger than myself, and I had no power over it as I had imagined I would. I think I was in love with you before I saw you. Certainly I have known it from the moment we met that we were destined for each other.

"If you go away from me now, you will be making the biggest mistake of your life, for having known you I shall never love again. Oh, darling, if you could guess how much!" Raoul held out his arms to her. "*Mignonne!*"

Caroline could not move for her feet seemed rooted to the ground. She no longer doubted his sincerity, but it was difficult to give in. She could only stare at him fascinated. She felt numb.

Raoul smiled sadly and dropped his arms. Caroline was not ready to give herself to him. Perhaps she was shy, or still afraid...? There was a detachment about her that made him feel anxious. Raoul sighed...

Then he said suddenly, as though he had remembered something, which might be a sort of ally to him: "I brought the third dress down in the box I put on the rack in the plane. Put it on for my mother to see before we return to Paris. It will please her so much."

"Have you seen it?" asked Caroline, but she was emotionally uncertain of herself, and said the first thing that came into her head. Then, suddenly, her face relaxed into a happy smile. It would give her great pleasure to try on a beautiful dress.

"No, but I have an idea what it is like, because I told Toinette my wishes. I never meant you to wear the last dress at the 'Maintenon'. It was to be worn for me. Now shall we go back?"

Caroline turned at once. Her mind was in a dither. Though Raoul had told her he loved her, and she had rejected him by making no answer at all, something warned her that nothing between them was finished. It was at the beginning. There was nothing for her to fear any more, for security was ahead of her. There was a solidity and endurance in the quality of the love he was offering her, a sure foundation for a happy marriage which

Caroline had always wanted in her dreams. What was happening was like a miracle…

They reached the Chateau in silence.

The Marquise was nodding on her stone seat in the sun. She had tired of waiting for them. Hers was the leisured existence of old age.

Raoul put his finger to his lips and crept past her, and smilingly, Caroline copied him.

The box was in the room where Caroline had been taken on her arrival.

"I will wait outside. Do not be long for our time is getting short," said Raoul.

He closed the doors and went over to a large bay window, and looked with unseeing eyes at the landscape, for his mind and heart were too full of Caroline to admit of anything outside that world.

Though Caroline did not take long to change, she was a long time in the room, and stood looking at herself in a big mirror, sure that she had never seen anything so radiant and entrancing as this lovely dress.

It was not black, or even sober, as Raoul had once said all three dresses must be. It was the pure white of a bridal dress.

Caroline knew that in wearing it she was telling Raoul she loved him. She was well aware why the dress had been given to her, and the occasion she was to wear it. She knew, too, what the Marquise would think when she saw her in this dress. Perhaps she already guessed how things were between them. Possibly the entire family were already aware of Raoul's romance.

As she recognized all this, it came to Caroline that nothing could ever have been different between them. As well try to stop Niagara as to stem the tide of their love for each other. It was all ordained by Fate when they were born. The thought made her feel happier than she had ever been.

Caroline heard Raoul say her name urgently, and she called out, "Coming," on a tremulous note. Softly she opened the door and waited on the threshold.

Raoul did not see her at once. He had gone back to his post at the window, and stood with his back to her, his hands clasped behind him — waiting.

"Raoul!"

He turned sharply and came towards her, his eyes, as they took in the beautiful vision standing in the open doorway, full of love and longing.

"You were gone so long, darling. I was afraid something had happened," he said anxiously in a low voice.

"I — was shy about coming out," she confessed.

"Shy of me, *mignonne?*" He took both her hands, but held her from him, his mouth soft and smiling, his eyes lit like lamps. "My wonderful darling! My beautiful!"

Swiftly he pulled her to him, his arms closing about her, and kissed her lovingly and passionately.

They remained thus for a long while. The world about them, the Marquise, the Château and the valley — everybody and everything had no existence, for they were enjoying the first favours of Paradise.

A NOTE TO THE READER

If you have enjoyed the novel enough to leave a review on **Amazon** and **Goodreads**, then we would be truly grateful.

Sapere Books is an exciting new publisher of brilliant fiction and popular history.

To find out more about our latest releases and our monthly bargain books visit our website:
saperebooks.com

Made in the USA
Monee, IL
10 April 2020